"I'm a makeup artist, not a confidence trickster."

"There's a difference?" he said with a sneer.

"I'm not interested in your money. Nor am I interested in *you*."

"Did I say that?"

' "*Without wishing to sound conceited, I can tell when a woman is interested—and she was*," ' she said, mimicking his voice. "Well, here it is, straight from the horse's mouth. She *wasn't*."

"I don't believe you," he murmured. And then he leaned forward and kissed her.

ANN CHARLTON wanted to be a commercial artist but became a secretary. She wanted to play the piano but plays guitar instead, and she never planned to be a writer. From time to time she abseils, which surprises her because she is afraid of heights. Born in Sydney, Ann now lives in Brisbane. She would like to do more tapestry work and paint miniatures and has absolutely no plans to research a book in the Amazon or to learn to play the bouzouki.

Books by Ann Charlton

HARLEQUIN PRESENTS
857—AN IRRESISTIBLE FORCE
912—TITAN'S WOMAN
967—THE DECEPTION TRAP
1008—STREET SONG
1319—LOVE SPIN
1777—HOT NOVEMBER

HARLEQUIN ROMANCE
2684—NO LAST SONG
2701—WINTER SUN, SUMMER RAIN
2762—THE DRIFTWOOD DRAGON
2977—RANSOMED HEART

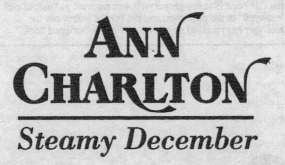

ANN CHARLTON

Steamy December

Harlequin Books

TORONTO • NEW YORK • LONDON
AMSTERDAM • PARIS • SYDNEY • HAMBURG
STOCKHOLM • ATHENS • TOKYO • MILAN
MADRID • WARSAW • BUDAPEST • AUCKLAND

ISBN 0-373-11782-5

STEAMY DECEMBER

First North American Publication 1995.

Copyright © 1995 by Ann Charlton.

This edition published by arrangement with Harlequin Books S.A.

® and TM are trademarks of the publisher. Trademarks indicated with
® are registered in the United States Patent and Trademark Office, the
Canadian Trade Marks Office and in other countries.

Printed in U.S.A.

CHAPTER ONE

UNTIL the two, large, uniformed officers showed up there was nothing about the job to actually alarm her.

'Just a few hours, that's all I'm asking,' her mother had said. 'Standing on a street, asking questions, with a tape-recorder in your bag.' Her mother ran a part-time employment agency and was always looking for students and out-of-work actors for all manner of odd jobs. As she had forged a new career in theatrical make-up and special effects, it was some time since Ami had been an out-of-work actor but she hadn't yet figured a way to remove her name from her mother's files.

'What kind of questions—and isn't that illegal? Recording people's answers without their knowledge?'

'Only if you record their names as well, darling,' her mother had said impatiently. 'It's for my freelance writer, who's doing research for a book and he's got a list of questions to ask—nothing dreadful, just "excuse me, have you got the time" and "do you know where I can catch a bus to Balmain" and so on. He wants a young, attractive woman who has no nerves about chatting to strangers, so naturally I thought of you. I'm trying to talk him into coming to the charity art show next week. Did I mention he's thirtyish, good-looking and divorced?'

'What kind of book?' Ami asked, picking her way through the minefield of Lenore Winterburn's marital aspirations for her only child.

'It's a long story,' her mother had said, not noticing her own pun as usual. 'Look, darling, I just don't have anyone else on the books at the moment who can do it

5

and you know how I hate letting clients down. Let Helen run the shop without you and do this little job for me and you won't be sorry.'

But Ami was feeling her first real twinge of regret when one of the large, uniformed men planted himself on the pavement in front of her and said, 'Afternoon, madam. We'd like a word.'

Ami glanced at the insignia on his sleeve. Not a policeman but a private security guard. She relaxed. 'Which word would you like?' she asked breezily and got a humourless stare.

'Perhaps we could talk inside?' A beefy hand indicated the glittering, glassed foyer of the near-completed Avalon Hotel, outside which workmen were laying marble on a walkway rimming the semicircular concourse. The hotel motto, *Come home to heaven*, was scripted in gold and white by the doors. Several life-sized bronzes of voluptuous women torchbearers on plinths lined the pathway to heaven. A sign informed passersby that these had been reclaimed from the nineteenth-century hotel demolished to make way for this new one, a token piece of conservation that had not impressed those who had protested against the change.

Ami frowned. 'Talk about what?'

'Come along now, don't play dumb. You've been warned once. We don't want any trouble, do we?' the second guard said, holding out a hand as if to take her arm.

Suddenly glad there were plenty of people around, Ami sidestepped and raised her voice. 'I don't know what you mean. Please go away.'

They seemed sensitive to the attention of bypassers, for the two men took a long look at her, then retreated in the direction of the hotel. Uneasily aware of the tape-recorder in her bag, she considered moving away but then, why should she? Ami turned and saw the guards in conversation with someone inside the Avalon's glass doors before passing pedestrians blocked her view. Next time she turned around, she came face to face with exactly the kind of man she was supposed to approach for her mother's writer client.

Thirty to forty age group. The cut of the suit indicated upper income bracket, businessman or professional. He met her eyes very directly and Ami blurted out the opening question she'd asked all the others.

'Excuse me, can you tell me the time?'

She assessed him with quickening interest. Tall, wide-shouldered, a lean body and a lean face, coal-black hair, near black brows dead straight as if drawn with a ruler. Wide mouth, almost as straight as the brows but unexpectedly full at the corners as if his lips had been drawn in by someone who hadn't wanted to stop. A face designed by an architect with a longing to paint. He had grey eyes, thickly and darkly lashed and in another man this might have produced a boyish, smiling impression. But the eyes were shrewd, assured, coolly calculating and cancelled out any mellowing effect from their lush framing.

'You must be a non-smoker,' he said easily.

'I'm sorry?'

'Isn't the standard gambit to hold out a cigarette and ask for a light?'

It conjured up a somewhat tawdry image. 'Maybe I really *do* just want to know the time,' she suggested gently, showing her wrists bare of a watch.

'If you really *did* just want the time, you would have noticed the hotel clock,' he said mockingly and turned a hawkish profile toward the unfinished hotel lobby where an art clock was clearly visible through the glass. He looked at her, lowered his chin and raised his brows, as if to say, 'Your move.'

Challenged, Ami promptly shaded her eyes and squinted. 'Oh, is there a clock? I haven't got my glasses,' she improvised, giving him a brilliant smile.

He blinked, looked deep in her eyes like an eye specialist diagnosing the exact nature of her vision impairment. Then he scrutinised her from her heeled boots all the way up her jeans to the jumble of blue alphabet letters knitted into her cream cotton sweater. His gaze lingered, as if he suspected there might be a complete word to be found there on her chest.

He consulted an expensive watch. 'Six-fifteen,' he said. 'Are you—waiting for someone in particular or...?'

Her heartbeat quickened. Was he going to try to pick her up? She was conscious of a dual excitement and repugnance at the idea. He waited with intense interest for her answer and she began to feel she was playing in some kind of competition. Or was being played with. Unsettled, she fell back on another of the routine questions she'd been asking. 'Do you know where the Bondi Junction buses leave?'

Whatever he'd been expecting her to say, that wasn't it. His eyebrows shot up. 'Lost your nerve?' he asked softly. 'Maybe you know who you're dealing with?'

Puzzled, Ami said again, 'Sorry?'

He beckoned her to follow, walked past a sculptured torchbearer to point to the bus terminal less than half a block away on the opposite side of York Street. 'If it's a Bondi bus you want,' he said sardonically, 'there's one.'

'No, that's going to Clovelly,' she said, easily reading the destination on the distant bus.

'It's a miracle,' he drawled.

'What is?'

'Your eyesight restored after mere moments in my company. And without me even laying hands on you.'

She felt a decided frisson at that. Involuntarily she looked at his hands. One was relaxed, by his side. The other was spread casually on the voluptuous, bronzed leg of the statue on the dais beside him. His thumb rubbed at the cast impression of a sandal strap.

'I've been watching you. From my office up there,' he said. Startled, Ami looked up at the mirrored blankness of the glass he indicated.

'My security thought at first that you might be casing the place for a robbery or terrorist action,' he went on conversationally.

My office, my security. His fingers flexed on the lavish curves of the torchbearer's calf muscle as if he relished the smooth perfection of the surface. Ami found it immensely annoying.

'I'm North Kendrick,' he went on smoothly. 'I own this place—more or less.'

And that included the statues, Ami thought, dragging her eyes from the proprietarial hand on the bronze. North? Was that a name or a compass bearing? A woman emerged from the hotel doors and signalled to him with a portable phone. Kendrick made a peremptory gesture that said, 'Wait.'

'Did you say terrorists?' Ami said, distracted.

'A bit extreme, I agree, although we had our troubles with SOPS during demolition of the old Avalon.' At her blank expression he said blandly, 'Save Old Pubs Society. Sometimes security overreacts.'

'Obviously. I'm no threat to your security.' She smiled, made a palms-up, hands to the side gesture that said, 'Look—no weapons,' in case he had his armed guards about to close in on her.

'I'm not so sure about that,' he murmured, eyes narrowed on her expansive gesture and smile. 'But then they realised you'd been here before. Working alone this time, are you? Isn't that unusual?'

'Why would that be unusual—what do you mean, *this time*?'

'There's a description of you on file, right down to the alphabet sweater.'

'A *description*? Well, it isn't of me! I've never seen your security men before.'

'They weren't the ones on duty before. And the probability of two long-legged women with blonde hair, pants and an alphabet sweater choosing my hotel as a, shall we say rendezvous is very slight.'

Ami's eyes flashed. There was clearly some confusion, and she could explain why she was here easily enough. But, she thought stubbornly, why should she have to explain herself to a series of officious, self-important, patronising males? 'First your guards, now you. This is verging on harassment, you realize.'

He looked admiring. 'You've got class, they didn't mention that in the files. Nor did they mention your eyes.'

Ami blinked. 'What?'

'I suppose you're wearing coloured lenses—that aquamarine colour can't be the real thing.'

'Can't it, indeed?' she said coldly.

For a moment he looked dubious, but his eyes flicked down to the letters on her sweater and whatever they spelled out for him restored his cool assurance. 'The thing is, I can't have prospective customers being—ah, canvassed right outside my doors. It might give the Avalon a bad name and my investors wouldn't like it. Spread the word, there's a good girl.'

'I haven't been a girl for at least ten years,' she snapped.

'I won't ask how long it is since you've been good.' His mouth twitched at his own wit. He took her arm in a deceptively casual grip.

'Now, just one minute!' Ami pulled back in alarm, but failed to dislodge him.

He raised a hand to the woman waiting at the doors for him. The woman said something into the phone. He nodded to the commissionaire. The man walked out and signalled a cab. 'I want you to let go of my arm,' she said, but the traffic surged and her voice was diminished and the summoned taxi swept in alongside. Ami couldn't believe it when Kendrick guided her strongly toward it.

'I don't *want* a cab, thank you,' she said loudly. 'I don't exactly know what you're talking about but if you at least let me—'

'Have it your way,' he said, not relinquishing his hold on her. 'You're probably just a nice girl selling magazine subscriptions but I'd prefer you didn't do it here. Or inside my hotel once it opens, for that matter. It's been most enjoyable, but I'm pressed for time so why don't we just leave it at that? No hard feelings, hm?'

'This is a public space—you have no right to hustle me away.'

'There might be some argument as to who's doing the hustling, sweetheart,' he said, amused. He crooked his index finger. The woman hurried over to hand him the phone. He turned his head and nodded. A limousine crept into view.

'Hustling?' she said frostily. The finger crooked again. The doorman hurried over, straightening his tie, adjusting the flower in his lapel. Without taking his eyes off her or releasing his hold, Kendrick spoke over his shoulder to the doorman. 'This lady has made a mistake, Morgan. She finds herself in the wrong place. Should she lose her way again, you will be good enough to show her into a cab.'

'Yes, Mr. Kendrick.' The doorman studied Ami. 'I never forget a face.'

'This is ridiculous!' Scarlet-faced, she tried to open her bag to show him the tape-recorder and her business card but Kendrick took her by the wrist and steered her into the cab while he spoke into the phone. The grip had all the charm of a handcuff, as she found when she tried to shake it off. The driver gawped insolently, the workmen stopped to watch as she was deposited in the cab. Her face flamed in humiliation. The man called Kendrick handed back the phone and leaned in. His eyes were piercing, intense, and Ami found the cab's interior suddenly suffocating.

'Sydney's a big place. Don't come back. I'm being nice about it this time but I don't like complications, understand?' He hesitated, eyes roaming over her face and hair. 'Life's tough, I know,' he said. 'It's nothing personal, sweetheart.' Then he turned and plucked the gardenia from Morgan's lapel. Ami recoiled as he leaned in again, a knee on the seat. The scent of the single flower was as overpowering as the looming presence of the man. He tucked the flower behind her ear. His fingers brushed against her cheek, and softly down the length of her hair. His gaze went to her mouth and he moved forward, tilted his head. Ami's mouth parted, she stared at him, held in a trance state as his breath mingled with hers. But he drew back a fraction just when she was certain he was about to kiss her. His hand curved around her jaw, his thumb stroked across her lower lip in a substitute kiss. Under his breath, he said, 'What a pity.' With that he closed the door and slapped twice on the roof of the taxi, which pulled away in slavish obedience. Kendrick got into the limousine and the two cars were briefly alongside each other before they entered the York Street traffic and she had one last glimpse of Kendrick's black hair and hawkish profile. She snatched the gardenia from her hair, ground it into a fragrant pulp with her heel, cursing that she'd left it too late for Kendrick to see what she thought of his patronising gesture.

'What a pity!' Ami mimicked to her best friend nearly two weeks later as she pulled off her grey wig in one of the Shoelace Theatre's dressing rooms. 'As if I was a— nice bit of sculpture he wouldn't mind putting with his half-naked bronzes, if only he hadn't found out it was flawed. Supercilious swine.'

'Well, if anyone can set a supercilious swine straight, it's you,' Emma said as she stacked up the metal chairs recently vacated by a dozen students. 'That was a terrific class. My workshop people were quite inspired.'

Ami didn't answer. That was the trouble. She hadn't set him straight at all. She thought of the spineless way she'd just sat there in the taxi and let that man tuck the flower in her hair, touch her face... every bit as inanimate as one of his bronze torchbearers, she thought, hating herself.

'Are you intending to drive home in full make-up?' Emma enquired. 'You look older than my grandmother. I'm having second thoughts about you being my bridesmaid.'

She indicated Ami's face, used to demonstrate her latex ageing effects, which had turned her into a seventy-year-old woman in around ninety minutes. But Ami looked broodingly in the mirror, not seeing her own made-up reflection. If it hadn't been for the gardenia, she thought, she would have forgotten the whole thing by now. She doubted she would ever again be able to smell the perfume of a gardenia without triggering off the memory of her humiliation. If only she had thrown the flower at him, she would feel so much better.

'Ami?'

Ruefully, she smiled. Emma was back from a brief reunion with her fiancé at his place out west, glowing with happiness and confidence, serene about her wedding plans and keen to talk about material samples and designs. 'Sorry to sound off but I just cannot abide that smug, superior kind of male. Didn't give me a chance to explain, just hustled me into a cab saying it had been "most enjoyable". And there was the gardenia and I thought for a moment he was going to... I should have bitten his thumb off,' she said blackly.

'His *thumb*?'

'His sniffy doorman studied me as if I was on the ten most wanted list and I'm banned from going inside that fancy hotel of his—can you believe it? "Sydney's a big place,"' she said in mimicry of Kendrick's deep voice. '"Don't come back."' She swept up an armful of used tissues and cotton-wool pads to toss them in the waste-bin and looked reflectively at Emma. 'When I was a kid, if someone told me I wasn't allowed to walk on the grass, I just *had* to go and put at least one foot on it.'

Emma's brows went up. 'You're not thinking of putting a foot on Kendrick's turf, are you?'

Ami grinned. 'I just might, at that.'

Her friend looked suddenly alert. 'North Kendrick? CKC? Electronics and transport and all the rest? I've heard about him. Hard as nails and twice as sharp. I'd sleep on the idea if I were you. Your pride might not withstand being thrown out a second time and I wouldn't gamble on the doorman not recognising you. Come on, take off your wrinkles. I keep thinking I'm talking to a stranger.'

Ami focused at last on her reflection. She blinked to centre the cloudy contact lenses that turned her eyes from aquamarine to an indeterminate grey-blue. The slight ir-ritation they caused gave her eyes a convincing watery look. With professional pride she prodded at the lifelike folds on her neck, the pliable, sagging jawline unde-tectable from real skin even for close television camera work. 'It *is* good, isn't it?' she said, pleased with her creation.

'Your own mother wouldn't know you. I'm going to lock up.'

'I hate to simply take it all off after so much work,' Ami complained, raising her voice as her friend disap-peared to check the exits and alarms of her theatre. 'It seems such a waste of effort.'

Ami sat, a finger teasing at the pins holding her long, blonde hair close to her scalp. Then, thoughtfully, she put on the grey wig again and adjusted it, leaning close to scrutinize the countenance her own mother wouldn't recognize.

Don't come back.
I never forget a face.
There's a description of you on file.

Ami's eyes gleamed. A smile played around her mouth. Such a *terrible* waste to simply dismantle ninety minutes of work. Waste not, want not, she thought virtuously.

'Emma,' she yelled, unzipping her cranberry jumpsuit. 'Can I borrow some gear from your costume department?'

The Avalon was open for business, its semicircular drive completed and lined with a row of potted, pollarded fig trees that looked like three-dimensional lollipops. Sydney's pigeons had discovered the torchbearers; there was a spattering of white on the smooth, bronze breasts and shoulders.

The suave watchdog, Morgan, once again wore a gardenia on his lapel. The man who never forgot a face looked blankly at her as she approached, and Ami felt the flush of elation she always got from a convincing piece of work. Emma's theatre costume department had yielded a floral dress and a cheap pink cardigan, support shoes, a vinyl handbag and white gloves. 'I shouldn't be helping you with this—it's a mad idea,' Emma had said, but she had been in theatre even longer than Ami and hadn't been able to resist the professional challenge of transformation. Body pads and a hunch had modified Ami's tall, dancer's body into a shorter, dumpier shape. Morgan had no more luck identifying her figure than her face.

'Can I help you, madam?' he said.

'I'm going to have a look at your lovely new hotel,' she confided cosily, taking pleasure in looking him right in the eye. 'And have a cup of coffee in your coffee shop.'

Morgan quickly reviewed her weathered wrinkles, her modest clothes, and his manner became more familiar. 'It's not a good time for that tonight, dear. It's an official opening, you see, for VIPs and the press—'

'That's all right, I don't mind a few officials,' she said broad-mindedly, suspecting that Morgan was trying to keep her out for an entirely new reason. She felt a jolt at the information. Kendrick was bound to be here if the place was crawling with VIPs and press. Just for a moment, she hung back. Emma was right, it was a mad idea. But the scent of Morgan's gardenia wafted to her nostrils and when he turned away with a toothy welcome for better-dressed people, Ami slipped through the doors.

Amongst the guests she recognized a media sports celebrity and a retired politician whose make-up she'd done once for a TV talk show. With the sports celebrity was a girlfriend wearing glamour-punk black and glitter, and with the politician a bow-tied, distinguished husband. All the beautiful people.

Morgan and his boss, she thought, would no doubt prefer not to have impoverished old ladies in pink cardies tottering around the lavish foyer spoiling the classiness of the place while the VIPs were present. Too bad. She intercepted a waiter who dubiously gave her a glass of champagne.

Through a gap in the crowd, she saw Kendrick. His tall, lean figure was distinguished in the black and white of a dinner suit. Were his shoulders really so broad? Probably overstuffed shoulder pads. A very elegant brunette, wearing fuchsia pink and pearls, stayed close by him as he greeted guests and journalists. He smiled and made an expansive gesture as he related some anecdote to his immediate audience. They all laughed. Well, they would, wouldn't they, she thought, remembering the obedient leap of the taxi when Kendrick had signalled it to go.

Kendrick, she had read since he had sent her packing, was success personified. He was into electronics, transport, property and a multitude of profitable ventures that had sprung from an unlikely start as an engineer with a handful of patented designs. He was one of just a few of the young turks who had avoided the financial quicksand of the past decade, known for a combination of flair, ruthlessness and a formidable patience for long-term investment. The only extravagant mistake he might have made, according to the financial pages, was to build this hotel. But a man with his resources could afford a mistake. Being on his turf seemed suddenly not only childish but dangerous. Ami couldn't have explained it, but she usually went with her intuition, so she was already plotting her course to the door through the cocktail dresses and the dinner suits when a young man wearing a hotel badge took her elbow and said softly, 'Good evening, madam. Allow me to call you a cab.'

Leaving was exactly what she'd intended but when she found herself being inexorably assisted to do so, she was nettled. When she glanced over and saw North Kendrick frowning in her direction, no doubt watching to see that she was removed, her temper flared. One way or another, he was always throwing her out. 'Oh, but I don't want to go yet,' she said in a quavering voice that nevertheless projected nicely in the soaring vestibule. 'I want to have a look around your lovely hotel.'

The young man beside her pasted an embarrassed smile on his face and moved her through the guests. She raised her voice a bit.

'Young man, you're hurting my arm. I don't understand why I'm being treated like a criminal just because I wanted to have a look around.'

Kendrick was looking over now with sharpened interest. So were several members of the press. Australians loved an underdog. Ami warmed to her role.

'Do you have to be rich and famous to come in to look at this hotel?' she asked the nearest guests. 'I couldn't stay here—couldn't afford that, not on the pension. But just to *look*—' The sentence remained pathetically unfinished. By now there was a decided pall over the celebrations. Kendrick had stopped smiling. Ami was beginning to enjoy herself. 'Tossed on the scrap heap,' she said with perfect clarity and a hint of tears because the contact lenses were hurting. 'That's all right. I'll go,' she said with a sniff. She was rather keen to make that exit now because Kendrick was approaching through the crowd, a frown deeply etched on his brow. He was perturbed, embarrassed because his guests were embarrassed. Good. Ami felt justice had been done and moved to the door with a vigour that took her escort by surprise.

It was Kendrick who stopped her, just as the massive glass doors slid apart. He carried with him an almost full glass of champagne but must have moved like greased lightning without spilling a drop, a fact that doubled her apprehension. 'Just a moment.' He gave her a clean white handkerchief, took her arm and handed the glass to the young man. 'Get someone to collect the current batch of champagne and replace it with properly chilled bottles. I like my champagne *cold*,' he said. The young man vanished on the command. Ami's glass of champagne had felt positively icy through her gloves. Kendrick was either a perfectionist or just liked throwing his weight around. 'I'm North Kendrick,' he said, bending toward her as she shrank into the hanky. 'I own this hotel and I apologise for any unpleasantness you might have encountered. The hotel management staff may have overinterpreted their instructions—'

What a lovely man, she thought. Dropping the blame on the staff who couldn't answer back. Ami felt the first real pangs of alarm as he led her inside the hotel as inexorably as his employee had been trying to lead her out. Wouldn't you know it, she thought furiously. The man wasn't going to risk the press writing up something unpleasant about a pensioner being ejected from the Avalon. Clasped to Kendrick's side, she felt near to panic.

'Will you tell us your name?' Kendrick bent persuasively over her. His beautiful brunette companion came over and introduced herself as Francesca quite loudly to Ami, assuming that deafness automatically went with wrinkles.

Ami saw that there was no way out of this. She could hardly take off her wig and admit she was a fraud. His gung-ho security guards would probably clap her in irons as a SOPS infiltrator. She would simply have to improvise until an opportunity to escape presented itself. 'My name is Amelia,' she said, giving the full version of her name she never used. She was rather disconcerted to find Kendrick's well-groomed head tilted an inch from her mouth. His skin was tan and rather rough-grained, his thick hair gleaming a Celtic black. Her gaze locked onto a single grey hair, shining like a tiny silver arrow just above his ear. Shifting her eyes from a close-up of his hair to a close-up of his resolute jaw, she almost gave him her real last name and hastily substituted an alias. 'Amelia Anderson,' she said. As soon as she said the name, she started concocting a personality for Amelia Anderson and she felt better. Safer. Or was that because North Kendrick had moved slightly farther away?

'Mrs. Anderson—it *is* Mrs?' he asked, glancing at her gloved left hand.

'I'm a widow,' Ami said cautiously.

'May I call you Amelia? You realise you've gatecrashed our opening celebrations, Amelia,' he said on a playful, yet chiding note.

If I really was seventy years old, she thought, I would strenuously object to being treated like a nincompoop. 'I didn't see any sign saying the public couldn't come in. I'm a gatecrasher because I'm not rich and important, isn't that what you mean, young man?'

Kendrick looked taken aback, an expression she felt was surely alien to him and that gave her some intense satisfaction. 'You are important, Amelia. In fact—' He paused and she could almost see the wheels turning as he assessed the situation. 'To mark our opening and your keen interest in the hotel—' It was said with the barest trace of dryness. 'We want you to be our guest for a weekend—absolutely free—in one of our best suites.'

Ami's horror was genuine. 'Oh, no,' she cried, as journalists took notes and photographers took pictures. 'I couldn't!'

Kendrick smiled slightly at this response. 'Of course you could. The doorman said you wanted to come in for a cup of coffee. Well, Amelia, you shall have all the coffee you can drink, on the house.'

It was clear that any little old lady in support shoes and a pink cardie should be jumping for joy at such largesse. As she acted overcome and flustered, her panic subsided. The whole thing had got out of hand, but why was she worried? Nobody knew who she was, the lighting was discreet enough for her latex to pass muster and people weren't looking all that closely at her. She was an old lady and everyone already thought they knew just what an old lady looked like so there was no need for close scrutiny. She would go along with this and simply fade away at the first opportunity.

The opportunity to escape didn't present itself. When she excused herself to go, ostensibly to the ladies room, Francesca went with her. Kendrick wasn't going to risk the now high-profile widow Anderson falling and breaking her hip on his premises. Fortunately, Francesca was too absorbed in touching up her own lovely face to notice that the widow Anderson didn't take off her gloves.

With relentless generosity, Kendrick included her in the tour of the grand new building. The press liked the quirky notion of the stray old pensioner being given the keys to a luxury suite. They demanded details. Where did she live? Was she alone in the world? Had she ever stayed in a luxury hotel before? She was shakily vague about her address and voluble about her family. 'Then there's my youngest son Bernard and my daughter-in-law, Brenda,' she waffled as the eyes of the press glazed over. 'And the grandkiddies...the twins, lovable, cheeky little devils.'

The party went up in the elevators, to tour the hotel's impressive function rooms, the ballroom, the restaurant and coffee shop. Champagne, spirits and canapés were offered at every stop. Ami, who had somehow been elevated to guest of honour, kept up a steady flow of appreciation.

'What a nice, *cosy* feel it has,' she said, of the standoffish chrome and marble interior of the coffee shop where the widow Anderson was destined to whoop it up during her stay. What would Kendrick do when the widow failed to turn up for her free holiday? 'But you know I can't help thinking a little lamp on every table would have just been the finishing touch. With a little, pleated shade on each of them, and maybe a tiny posy of artificial flowers. I make them, you know.' She beamed at a bemused North Kendrick who must surely be regretting his decision to include her in the party. 'Lamp shades. I must have made—oh, hundreds of lamp shades in my time.'

With this impressive feat to mull over, they moved on to the empty ballroom where, to Ami's dismay, chandeliers blazed. But, at a barely perceptible nod of Kendrick's handsome head, the lights dimmed and the great waltz from *Der Rosenkavalier* swelled through hidden speakers. No wonder Kendrick thought highly of himself—his passage through life was smoothed by people who just stood about waiting to do what he wanted, when he wanted, at a quirk of his eyebrow. The widow Anderson must have come as a nasty surprise, she thought maliciously.

'Oh, my,' said Ami clasping her gloved hands. 'How I used to love to waltz. I used to be quite a dancer in my time, but I don't suppose you believe that, Mr. Kendrick—or may I call you North?' she said roguishly.

'Waltz with me, Amelia,' North Kendrick said, holding out his arms. All the cameras went up in readiness. Francesca, who was a fashion designer, wearing her own creation, looked disappointed that this prime piece of exposure was going to someone with nothing to promote.

Ami's roguish smile disappeared. 'Oh, I couldn't— my *legs* aren't what they used to be. Dance with Francesca.'

'Just one circuit.' He smiled. What very good teeth he had, she thought, staring at him and cursing her impulsiveness. He moved in and there was nowhere to go but into his arms.

He was a reasonably good dancer. As one who had trained in ballet since four years old, she was inclined to judge harshly. Even so, he was very stylish, very crisp, very purposeful. It would be interesting to dance properly with him instead of this measured, sedate circuit of the floor suitable for a dowager. As the heady music swelled, quickened into a whirling pace, Ami wondered what would happen if she straightened out of her stoop, threw back her head and slid her hand around that rather interesting angle of his neck. The thought so startled her that she stumbled. His arm tightened in support and she was drawn up onto her toes through several bars of frolicking music, her false matronly bosom and the pink cardigan crushed to his chest, her mouth narrowly missing his bow tie.

'Are you all right, Amelia?'

Genuine concern had such an amazing effect on his uncompromising features that she stared unguardedly for a moment. His eyes narrowed. Ami's head filled with the drumbeat of her pulse. Had her contact lenses slipped? Oh, lord, why had she let herself get so carried away? The man would tear her limb from limb.

But he smiled and said, 'I'll bet you never lacked partners when you were a girl.'

'Well...' she said modestly, almost sagging in relief.

'Did your husband like to dance?'

'No,' she said, unwilling to complicate matters with a dancing husband. 'Most men don't have the first idea of dancing. Now *you*, North,' she said truthfully, 'you're a very good dancer. You know how to lead. So many men don't.'

He laughed. 'It's the age of equality, Amelia. A lot of women don't appreciate men who take control. Consequently men are less confident about taking the lead in anything lest they be labelled chauvinist pigs.'

Balderdash, she thought. 'Dear me. Well, I can see you don't let the age of equality bother you, North.'

His brows went up. She smiled seraphically though the strain of disguising her height, the heat of the wig and the padding and the latex were getting to her. Her heartbeat was galloping along at a pace that would surely make him call an ambulance if he felt the vibrations. But moments later, smiling as the guests applauded, he led her from the floor. She ought to send him a bill considering the public relations value he was getting out of Amelia Anderson, she thought sourly.

A man in a wheelchair had joined the guests while she was dancing, Ami noticed. He was elderly and very thin, with a face like a creased leather satchel and large hands with knobby knuckles and wrists. A superb dark suit sat awkwardly on him, as if he was done up in someone else's Sunday best. North Kendrick looked displeased at the man's presence and went to him at once, bending over him to say a few words. The old man shook his head and settled into the chair with an air of stubbornness. If he'd been asked to leave, he wasn't going, either. Kendrick had his share of out-of-place senior citizens tonight, Ami thought, catching the eye of the invalid. He looked tired but his gaze was unexpectedly sharp, and she nodded and turned away quickly, unwilling to be examined by a genuine elder. Ami found those eyes focused steadily on her as she was held in conversation by various people and forced to expand on her family life. She exhausted Bernard and the twins and launched her eldest son, Duncan, who lived in Canada. Something about the watchful old man was disturbingly familiar, and she felt a new urgency to get away. But no sooner the thought than North Kendrick was there, taking her arm again and steering her to the disabled man. Were old women always bundled around in this bossy manner?

'Amelia, meet my father,' he said. 'Harry Kendrick.'

His father? She was taken aback but the sense of familiarity was explained. The man's eyes were like his son's except there was a gleam in them to suggest humour to match the shrewdness.

'How do you do, Mr. Kendrick,' she said carefully.

The old man listened as his son explained Amelia's presence and her expected stay in a penthouse suite as a guest of the management. 'Is that so?' Harry said, raising shaggy eyebrows. 'And is there a Mr. Anderson?'

'Amelia is widowed, too, Harry,' North said.

Ami had the sudden crazy thought that Kendrick might be matching her up with his dad. She almost burst into hysterical laughter. Harry was asking her about her family, and she went into her patter about her elder son, Duncan, who lived in New Zealand. As soon as she said it she knew she'd made a slip. Duncan lived in Canada. She started to feel a bit desperate.

'Nice place, New Zealand. A lot like Canada, I believe,' Harry said blandly and gave her a wink. Just then there was a concerted move to another location and he patted a chair alongside him and said, 'Sit down and take a load off your feet for a while, Mrs. Anderson.'

It was an ideal opportunity to escape. She sat down, not certain whether she'd been rumbled. When Kendrick and the crowd disappeared, she counted to ten, but instead of leaving, she turned to meet Harry's watery, blue-grey eyes. They were crinkled up in silent laughter.

'If you're a pensioner, I'm the prime minister,' he said.

CHAPTER TWO

SHE could have gone then. Kendrick might come back at any moment. But professional curiosity delayed her. 'What gave me away?'

Harry drew a handkerchief from his suit pocket and wiped his eyes. 'Oh, never mind. You're not one of those SOPS people, are you? Is there a bomb in that handbag?'

'Good heavens, is everyone in this place paranoid about bombs?' she said lightly, opening her bag to show him that it contained no explosives. She spun him a tale about wanting to test out her special effects in public, which was, after all, close to the truth. 'They were so good,' she said modestly, 'that one thing led to another and—here I am.'

'And North doesn't have a clue!' Harry went off into wheezy laughter again. 'Ah, this is a rare treat. He's a smart lad, you see, smarter than me. I never had much education, worked with my hands all my life, on building sites around the city. Nowadays people like my boy knock down things I helped to build and replace them with fancy towers like this,' he said with a sigh as he squinted out the window at the glittering city. 'North, now—he was brainy right from the start, was rich before he turned thirty. People have been bowing and scraping to him, treating him like a god for so long, it's no wonder he thinks he knows everything.' He went off again, gasping and heaving. 'My poor boy! I think he was hoping to do a bit of matchmaking between me and the widow!' He mopped up again and she was watching him stuff the handkerchief in his top pocket when his other hand flashed out and plucked the wallet from her open bag.

26

It was unfolded and he was reading her business card before she gathered her wits.

'Ami Winterburn,' he read out loud. 'Performing Arts, Special Effects, Peruke Maker, Illusion—Theatrical Supplies. Busy girl, aren't you? What's a peruke?'

'A wig,' she said, swiping her wallet from him.

'And what's Illusion? A shop or something?'

She took the card and tucked it away, not answering.

He had retained her driver's licence and now checked her date of birth. 'Hm. Twenty-six. Single?'

'Yes. You're a nosy old man,' she said, dismayed that he'd seen her real name. Amelia Anderson could just fade into the blue. Ami Winterburn, failed actress, make-up artist and wigmaker, was listed in bold type in the phone book.

'And you're a fraudulent old bag,' he guffawed, surrendering the licence. 'It's my birthday today. I'm seventy-one.'

'Well, happy birthday.'

He grinned at her tension. 'Don't worry. I won't tell North your real name,' he said and as she relaxed, added, 'but only if you stay and come to the penthouse in that get-up to celebrate my birthday.'

'That's blackmail,' she squeaked.

'That's right, Mrs. Anderson.'

Head flung back, she stalked to the door, forgetting the frock and the pink cardigan and the stout shoes. Harry looked on with appreciation.

'Bet you're a good-looking woman under all that. But that won't cut any ice with North if he finds out what a fool you've made of him. He's not a man who likes to be messed about.'

'You wouldn't tell him?'

But Harry just grinned, and she'd passed up her chance at escape because North Kendrick came back just then, with Francesca and the others following in the high good humour generated by alcohol and pampered egos.

'North, my boy—Mrs. Anderson's got a surprise for you,' Harry announced, with a provocative look at Ami. Horrified, she thought he really did intend to get his birthday kicks by exposing her in front of everyone. She imagined peeling off her disguise to stand before Kendrick, imagined those grey eyes on her real face. Her nerve broke.

'I'm, er, Harry kindly invited me to celebrate his birthday with you tonight,' she twittered. 'Unless of course I would be intruding on a family occasion—'

North broke in quite eagerly to assure her she wouldn't be intruding. Francesca wouldn't be staying for dinner, but would escort them up and he would join them when his guests had gone. Ami thought she saw the whites of Francesca's eyes at this, but the woman accompanied them dutifully.

The penthouse was sheer luxury. In the mellow light of table lamps, a pale lake of marble stretched out with clustered furniture on islands of rugs. Sculptures in bronze and stone, mirrored in the marble, looked like ancient monuments stranded in water. A clump of prehistoric palm-like cycads flourished beneath a domed skylight. Softly lit shelves set into the walls housed a host of art treasures. A table was set for dinner with candelabra and on a trolley was a large, perfect birthday cake covered in candles. Ami thought there would be exactly seventy-one. It was all tasteful, perfect, elegant. It had the touch of the hotel's catering department on it. Impersonally yours, she thought, remembering that brief glimpse of irritation tonight when North Kendrick had first seen his father. She wondered what he had given Harry for his birthday. A diamond-studded tie clip or something equally fabulous, she supposed.

Francesca was drawn to a panoramic mirror where she anxiously surveyed her lovely face.

'Mirror, mirror on the wall,' Harry muttered with a grimace. 'You don't think he'd marry her, do you?'

Ami studied Francesca anew at this idea. She wasn't sure which one she would pity most in such a liaison. But she didn't answer, and Harry reached out and touched the wrinkles at the corner of her eyes, smiling smugly at the success of his manouvres.

'Dirty Harry,' she whispered from the corner of her mouth. 'I'm not accustomed to being blackmailed into doing things.'

'Ah, my days as a blackmailer are numbered. Can't count on another birthday after this one.'

She was disconcerted. 'You mean that you're...?'

Harry gave a philosophical shrug and a gaunt grin that cut to the heart of her. She must be mad but in spite of everything, she liked this reprehensible old man who seemed so lonely in this elevated bastion of good taste. 'Well,' she said. 'Just keep your part of the bargain. And make sure that the lights stay down low. I don't want to be unmasked over the birthday cake.'

North Kendrick arrived then, emerging suddenly from behind the clump of cycads, shedding his dinner jacket, satisfaction tilting his mouth, a gleam in his eyes. He had turned a potential difficulty into an advantage, the evening had been a success and he had the look of a winner. There was a symbolic warning here somewhere, Ami thought, that in this haven of sophistication the man should appear, triumphant, from behind a lush growth of plants that dated back to primitive times. He tossed the jacket onto a couch, and rolled up the sleeves of his evening shirt. The overall impression was of broad-shouldered athleticism. Of course, his leanness could be mere skinniness. Under that loose, expensive shirt he was probably thin as a rake, his ribs sticking out.

'Amelia,' he said, stretching his hands toward her. 'I can't tell you how pleased I am you're joining us.' His warmth made her uneasy, guilty. But she thought of his enthusiasm to have a complete stranger join in a family affair and wondered if it was relief. Maybe, she speculated, North Kendrick just didn't want to be alone with his father. Her gloved hands were held in his and he stooped toward her, lingered for a moment, and she felt the draw of his attraction as his eyes crinkled with a smile. Old ladies, apparently, brought out a certain sweetness in Kendrick. He closed his eyes briefly, took a deep breath and Ami found herself gazing at him, fascinated by this uninhibited boyishness.

'That reminds me of my grandmother,' he said with a nostalgic sad-sweet smile that caught at her.

'What does?'

'That scent. What is it?'

'Oh. Just some talc,' she said weakly. At the theatre, she'd shaken some apple blossom talc on to disguise the smell of adhesive, and she was jolted that her fraud had brought back an intimate memory to him. It seemed a very refined form of cheating. Ami felt terrible.

North joined Francesca to fetch some drinks.

'The best birthday present of them all,' Harry said, watching his son. 'It's the first time since he was about fifteen that I know something he doesn't.' He positively glowed with his secret knowledge. Ami couldn't decide which was sadder—Harry's malicious pleasure at her presence, or his son's patent relief at it. She looked over at Francesca who appeared to be mixing more than drinks with North. The brunette rested her fingertips on the junction of his neck and shoulder, to emphasise some point. There must be something about that part of his neck that women liked. Ami thought of her own ridiculous fixation on it when she'd danced with him. Her fingertips tingled.

'What did you get for your birthday, Harry?' she said abruptly as she noticed the old man keenly observing her interest. 'Other than Amelia Anderson, I mean.'

Harry guffawed silently, reached down the side of the wheelchair and produced some birthday cards, made by his grandchildren. 'Here's a card from my neighbour—she's looking after my house while I'm staying here. North wants me to sell it, so I hope it will still be mine when I want to go back,' he said dryly.

She looked at him askance. 'You're joking, aren't you?'

'North likes to get his way,' the old man said with a stubborn set of his jaw that suggested where North's trait might have come from. 'He gave me this for my birthday,' he said, pushing back his shirt cuff and holding out his left hand. There was a gold Rolex watch on his knobby wrist. 'Shockproof,' the old man said, looking at the beautiful timepiece. 'And waterproof down as far as two hundred metres.' There was some gentle humour in his eyes as he raised them to Ami. 'Better make sure I don't lose my head and go diving deeper than that, eh?'

They were laughing when North brought the drinks. Francesca made some polite, expert small talk in a loud voice for the benefit of the old folks, then said goodbye and North saw her to the elevator. Through the cycad's palm-like fronds Ami caught a glimpse of Francesca clasped in his arms, or him being clasped in Francesca's, it was hard to tell. The goodbye kiss was brief, anything but passionate, probably because they had no privacy at present. As he came back Ami wondered what that was like—being kissed by North Kendrick. The adolescent speculation annoyed her.

Through dinner, Harry continued to extract the maximum enjoyment from the situation. Ami couldn't help feeling that although Harry might not have the money and power of his son, he was far from the helpless, pitiful old man he'd portrayed to her.

'North. Such an unusual name,' Ami said curiously.

'We named him Connaught—his mother's maiden name. Always intended to call him Connor, but as soon as he could talk he called himself Nort . . . it kind of grew into North. He insisted on it, refused to answer to Connor. Stubborn as a mule even when he was three,' Harry said in mingled irritation and pride.

Connaught. Ami glanced at North, who was taking all this chitchat about his babyhood with surprising tolerance. She pictured him a chubby child lisping his own name, insisting on his version of it. Harry produced baby pictures after dinner, passing them to Ami with a dry commentary guaranteed to wreck the image of a grown-up, successful son. There was one of a near-naked toddler on a beach, concentrating fiercely on shovelling sand into a bucket. There was a family shot of a dark-haired woman with North and an older girl, decorating a Christmas tree. 'We had one every year,' Harry said. 'There was this place we used to get our trees—don't suppose it's there anymore. Ah, take a look at this one.' It was a later photograph of North, sitting on the pillion seat of a Ducati motorbike clinging to a dashing, leather-clad Harry. At eight or nine, he was a thin boy showing little signs of the compelling looks he would have in maturity. His intelligent face bore an expression of mingled pride, confidence and anxiety. Ami wondered if the confidence had driven out all uncertainties or if the grown man had simply become more adept at disguising his inner doubts. A quick comparison with the adult North convinced her that this latter idea was unlikely. North Kendrick had the air of a man who had the answers and never doubted himself, whether he was buying a company or clearing the streets of unsuitable women.

'I used to race Cats. Ducati bikes,' Harry explained. 'Won quite a bit, too.' To his son Harry said gruffly, 'I don't suppose you remember much about that.'

North looked startled. 'Of course I remember, Harry,' he said so emphatically that Ami thought he was putting

on a front and had in fact consigned Harry's racing days
to the forgotten files. Ami wondered at what age North
stopped calling his father Dad, or if he ever had.

The birthday candles were lit and extinguished, the
cake cut and Ami said her goodbyes.

'I'll come down with you,' North said, steering her
into the lift. Her heart thumped.

'No, there's no need,' she said, desperate to escape at
last. But he pressed buttons and the lift doors closed on
Harry in his wheelchair, and she was alone with his son.

'Can you spare another few minutes, Amelia?' North
said as the elevator stopped on the mezzanine floor. He
gave her no time to answer, but guided her from the lift
and along a hushed, carpeted corridor to an office. Her
pulse was all but deafening now. He must know, and it
was even worse now, because she was beginning to quite
like him, and her guilt was killing her. Kendrick flicked
a switch, which turned on a desk lamp, an uplighter and
several discreet lights that illuminated paintings and an
elegant sculpture on a marble base. More like a miniature
art gallery than an office, she thought, bracing herself
as he stood before her, frowning, hands on hips. How
long had he known?

'I want your advice, Amelia,' he said.

She gaped at him.

'About Harry.'

He guided her into a low chair alongside a coffee table
and she leaned back, weak with relief, wondering how
much of this kind of stress she could take. He talked
about Harry's stubborn wish to go back to managing
alone in his own house instead of moving into more
suitable surroundings. It became clear that it wasn't
advice he wanted so much as simply to talk. It also
became clear that Harry had deliberately tugged at her
heartstrings with hints that he wasn't long for this earth.
He wasn't even permanently confined to a wheelchair,
according to his son, but recovering from an operation

on his knees. She gritted her teeth, remembering how moved she'd been by his assertions that there would be no more birthdays. That old phoney, she thought furiously. The irony of that hit her a moment later and she almost laughed.

'I haven't seen him so animated in weeks. He's been very—depressed, in fact, since the operations. You're good for him, Amelia. I hoped, if I could tell you the way things are, you might be able to get my point across to him when you see him again. You're his contemporary and I think he'd listen to you. After all, you must know many people whose health has forced them to reconsider their way of life.'

'Oh. Hm,' she murmured. So that explained North's affection for poor old Amelia. She might come in useful to bring Harry around to North's way of thinking. He certainly knew how to get a benefit out of everything that came his way. She liked him less and her conscience eased a little.

He waved his hand at a hotplate where a jug of coffee simmered. 'Coffee?'

She demurred and said, 'I really must go.'

'Just a few minutes, please,' he said with a natural smile of great charm. She studied him while he took a china cup from a cupboard and milk from a small refrigerator. When he was talking to her, believing her to be old, he seemed more relaxed, less guarded. She shifted a little to ensure that the lamp alongside did not illuminate her face. Her attention was drawn to a notebook and some invoices on the side table. All bore the imprint of Monica's Executive Gifts and a slogan that promised that Monica could take all the hassle out of gift buying for busy executives. Monica, it seemed, could 'personalise' the gifts so that the receivers would never know the giver hadn't set eyes on them. Maybe Monica had selected Harry's birthday present, she thought cynically.

North seated himself in his magnificent chair, a study of male rakishness as he lounged, drinking coffee, his hair black as night, his white shirt carelessly open and catching the light, his skin a burnished gold in the mellow highlights thrown by the lamp. Ami wondered just how busy he kept Monica's gift-buying service.

'My sister lives in Melbourne and has her hands full with four children and two stepchildren. Ideally, I should get married and have Harry live with me,' he said. 'As his contemporary, what do you think about that?'

'Married? To Francesca?' she asked, finding an awful fascination in the scenario. Sophisticated, ambitious North Kendrick, the narcissistic Francesca—and Harry?

His now rather heavy-lidded eyes settled on her. He smiled, more mellow than ever, and Ami remembered that he'd had two brandies after dinner. Alcohol certainly took the harsh edge off him. He looked sleepy and relaxed and almost cuddly. 'Do I detect a note of disapproval, Amelia?'

'Oh, goodness me. It's not my place to pass comment,' she said, genuinely flustered. 'But—'

He lifted his brows in query. 'But?'

'Well—I mean, does Francesca like that idea? Of having Harry living with you?'

'I haven't actually discussed it with her.'

'Have you proposed?' she asked, feeling a curious sympathy suddenly for the ornamental Francesca.

He let his head drop back on the chair and closed his eyes. 'Not yet. I'm only thinking about it.'

'Do you love her?' she said before she could stop herself.

His chest heaved with a silent laugh. 'Does that seem important to you, Amelia?'

'It helps,' she said tartly.

'I suppose I thought that eventually love would come my way, but...it hasn't.' He sighed. 'I'm thirty-five, Amelia. When I was young I was always ahead of my contemporaries, and now I'm still out of step. All my friends are married. I meet a lot of women but they are usually too young or too old, or ready to settle for any man with money. If they're not married they're divorced and neurotic, or they're feminist academics.' He finished with a shudder.

Poor man. The whole female sex was unsatisfactory.

'Francesca suits me in many ways. She's quite beautiful—as I'm sure you noticed. I frankly admit I prefer my women to be beautiful.'

Ami took some deep breaths. He preferred his women to be beautiful and his champagne cold.

'I've known Francesca and her husband a long time. She's separated and possibly faced with a messy divorce and she's happy to have an uncomplicated relationship, someone to be seen with. Her husband had an affair,' he explained. Ami wondered if that was the reason Francesca checked her appearance so often, with that slightly dazed air, wondering what she didn't have that the other woman had. 'We enjoy similar things—she likes entertaining and I have to do a lot of that. She comes to me for financial advice—I often find her contacts useful—'

A sort of corporate affair, Ami thought. They probably claimed each other as a tax deduction.

'You don't approve, I can see. You're a romantic, Amelia. Maybe you'd prefer to know that I can, and do, fall for the wrong kind of woman. I just don't allow it to develop.'

'A bit like frostbite stunting the growth of a new, little plant?' she said, with gentle spite.

He laughed. 'No point in letting something start when you know it can only be trouble in the long term. There was a case in point not so long ago, a woman who caught my eye...'

A woman who caught his eye, like a flashy car, or a nice sports jacket, Ami thought. 'But she was the wrong kind of woman? Tch, tch. Neurotic? Feminist? Or just not beautiful enough, North dear?'

He seemed amused and entertained by her sarcasm. 'She was lovely. I was instantly attracted to her.' He got up and went to the window. 'I saw her from here, in fact, not so long ago, but when I went down to talk to her...'

'She had a voice like a crow?' Amelia said before she registered what he'd said. Her eyes widened. *I saw her from here. I went down to talk to her.* She froze, looking at his back as he stood staring over the hotel forecourt and the street. He must mean *her.* The knowledge touched her vanity for a fleeting moment. *I was instantly attracted to her.* A flare of triumph was followed by distaste. In desperation, she cast around for escape, a trapped eavesdropper.

'Her voice was good, too. I doubt the colour of her eyes and hair was real, but apart from that there were no apparent flaws in her at all—but her circumstances were, shall we say, unsavoury.'

Ami's nostrils quivered. No *apparent* flaws, indeed. Her self-loathing was considerably reduced by this breathtaking arrogance.

'A pity. It might have been interesting.'

'She might not have fancied *you*, North, dear, have you thought of that?' she said.

He had not. 'Without wishing to sound conceited, Amelia, I can tell when a woman is interested,' he said with a smile of reminiscence. 'She was, and it wasn't just business.' He glanced at her then, as if regretting such a frank reference to an old lady, presumably sheltered from the knowledge of such things as prostitution.

'You can tell! Dear *me*,' she said, gripping her bag tightly. 'What a very handy knack that must be. How does it work?'

He blinked and gave a boyish, rueful laugh. 'I couldn't even attempt to explain it, Amelia. But let's just say, I had it on good authority that she was not the kind of girl Harry would like me to bring home to dinner, so I—passed up the opportunity.'

Ami clutched her handbag and resisted the urge to hit him with it. So, he thought she'd been interested but *he'd* passed up the opportunity because she wasn't up to snuff! The self-opinionated stuffed shirt. His phone buzzed and he went over to the desk.

'Yes?' he said, snapping out of his nostalgic mood. There were some curt monosyllables and she got up, seeing her chance to get away. North Kendrick looked over and she made fluttery little gestures of thanks and farewell.

But he said, 'Hold on,' laid the receiver on the desk and came over. Taking her by the arm again, he walked to the lift with her, asking if she required a car to take her home. Ami said hastily that she had her own, which surprised him a little. 'There have been a few incidents around here,' he said. 'I'll have Morgan walk you to your car.'

'Thank you.' She beamed. He was letting her go alone. Thank heavens. The elevator door closed. He was gone. She was safe.

Morgan was at the concierge's desk taking a call and she slipped out before he saw her. Ami let out a great sigh of relief. One more minute and she would have hit Kendrick. *I can tell when a woman is interested.* She realised she was swinging her handbag in a furious arc and hoisted it over her arm. Up there in his office Kendrick might be watching her now, wondering why the widow Anderson wasn't tamely being escorted to her car by Morgan. She walked a little faster, anxious to get to the intersection so that she could abandon her elderly pace and get out of here. She heard footsteps overtaking her and for a moment her guilty conscience made her think it might be Kendrick, about to unmask her.

She upped her pace a fraction but the footsteps gained on her just before she turned the corner, and with the accelerated sound came the first prickle of apprehension. She glanced around and saw a youth break into a run toward her. He grabbed her handbag, but the handle caught on her wrist and tightened painfully as he tried to bolt with it. She couldn't get away, so she jabbed him with her elbow and landed a kick on his legs.

'Ow! Let go, you old bag! What do you think you're doing?' There was a note of injury in his voice, as if she was breaking some unwritten code by hitting back at her attacker. He saw that her wrist was entwined with the handle and brutally jerked the handbag free. The force might have broken the arm of a seventy-year-old woman. But Ami Winterburn was twenty-six and strong from years of ballet training and she saw red.

'You horrible little creep!' she yelled, loping around the corner after him. 'Attacking old women! Coward!'

The purse snatcher looked around with disbelief as this particular old woman sprinted alongside and gave him a vigorous push. Alarmed at the aged virago snarling at him, he stopped and raised a clenched fist at her. Ami delivered a high ballet kick that ripped her skirt and connected just below his elbow. His mouth dropped open in pain and shock. He flung down the handbag and fled. 'Just think twice before you pick on old ladies, you coward!' she yelled after him and shakily bent to pick up a few things that had spilled from her bag. Still kneeling, she looked along the street and saw a man coming to her rescue, slowing now as it was obvious the danger was past.

She blinked. It was North Kendrick. As her pulse crashed thunderously faster in her ears, his steps grew slower still. She closed her handbag, stood up. From his window he must have seen the youth follow her. How much had he seen and heard of what came after that?

'Oh dear,' she said breathlessly enough, clutching the ripped skirt over her thigh, trying to shrug her body pads back into place. 'My dress—torn to shreds, that awful boy, thank goodness you're here, Mr. Kendrick. North.'

His dead straight eyebrows crammed together in a deep frown. 'Amelia?' he said. She made a move away but he snapped his arm around her, reflectively spread his hand at her waist as if remembering when he danced with her. Ami tried to lean away from him, and his eyes narrowed at the youthful flex of muscle he could feel between the displaced body pads.

'Oh, it was terrible, that awful boy—I'm shaking all over,' she said truthfully. 'And I've skinned my knee.'

She bit her lip, wishing she hadn't directed his attention there. His head tilted, he took a torn edge of her skirt and lifted it aside like a curtain. Even in the black support shoes her legs were the firm, shapely legs of a dancer.

'Who are you?' he said softly. He took her arm in a grip less tender than she'd been used to from him and hauled her up close. Her hands braced against his upper arms. It was a bad time to discover he was anything but thin. Hard muscle rippled beneath her fingers and Ami tried to console herself that North Kendrick was sure to have a sense of humour over this. He was bound to see how ridiculous the whole thing was and enjoy a good laugh. Given time, he might even appreciate just how good her make-up job was. And there was Harry. She'd made his father very happy on his seventy-first birthday, hadn't she?

Ami looked at his set jaw and the muscle twitching in his cheek and decided not to rely on his sense of humour.

'Oh, dear, dear,' she said in a flustered, distressed voice.

It was enough to shift the balance of power. North's reason was telling him one thing, but she could see he was hampered by the visual signals his brain was interpreting. Confused, he relaxed for a moment and didn't expect the strength behind the shove she gave him. Kendrick sprawled on the footpath, the second man that night she'd floored in that spot, she thought in panicky humour, and Ami sprinted past some baffled bystanders and turned the next corner into the back street where she'd parked her car. Panting, she took several stabs with the key and finally got the door open. Just in time, she got inside, closed the door and sank down below the dashboard as Kendrick appeared at the corner, looking for her fleeing figure. After maybe thirty seconds, she cautiously raised one eye and saw him walk a little way down, then back again as if he'd given up, and quite suddenly the street corner was deserted.

Ami breathed deeply, waited a good ten minutes for safety then started the car. She was so rattled, she took two wrong turns in the city and added a frustrating half hour to her journey. At home, she pulled off the ripped dress, the body pads, the support shoes and stockings, wrapped herself in a short, silk robe and made herself some strong coffee. Her dog, barricaded inside the back garden, barked a welcome and a demand for release and Ami yelled, 'Just a minute, Spritz.'

She put an adhesive strip over her skinned knee then pulled off the wig and tossed it on her dresser. When the doorbell rang, she jumped, sat frozen for a moment. 'Fool,' she muttered, going to answer the door. It would be Emma with sample fabrics for the wedding, wondering why she'd taken so long to drink a cup of coffee at Kendrick's hotel. She opened the door, talking as she unfastened the chain. 'You'll have to talk to me while I get this stuff off my face. My skin is absolutely—' She stopped with her mouth open.

It wasn't Emma. It was North Kendrick.

CHAPTER THREE

'IF IT isn't the widow Anderson,' he drawled, looking at her long, smooth legs displayed beneath the robe. 'Been paddling in the fountain of youth, Amelia?'

She tried to close the door, which was mad, because now that he knew where she lived, it was much too late. But he stuck his foot in the opening, laid one hand flat against the door and pushed it open, then walked past her.

'How did you—?'

'Find you?' he finished, walking over to peer into her kitchen, thrust aside the curtain of the dining nook. Coming back to her, he reached past and gave the door the merest nudge. It slammed behind her and once again she jumped. 'You left your card, Ms. A. Winterburn.' He tweaked a credit card from his shirt pocket and flicked it at her feet. Ami clutched the robe closer to her breasts and bent to pick up the card.

'It dropped from your purse during your free-for-all with the bag snatcher. At least Amelia appears to be your real name. That's something, I suppose.'

She licked her lips. 'Most people call me Ami. Look, I can explain—'

His mouth thinned and he turned a glacial look on her. When he was sure he'd frozen her to the spot he walked away, down the narrow hallway, looking into her bathroom, bedroom, her spare room with her make-up dresser and work-table with several partly finished wigs on forms. She wondered what he expected to find—a covey of old ladies? As he came back, he picked up one of the matronly shoes that she had discarded in the living room.

'The hotel has very good facilities for checking out suspect credit cards. You'd be surprised what I know about you now. Your business partnership, what you earn. What you *owe*.' He strolled all the way back, turning over the shoe and inspecting it closely before he tossed it onto a chair. Ami thought she should have heeded that warning earlier when he'd appeared from behind the primitive plant life in his apartment. 'Everything I need to know,' he went on. 'Except what you really look like.'

And when he knew that, he would be angrier still.

'So let's get the sweet, old wrinkles off, shall we?' he snapped, gesturing towards her spare room.

'You're not going to watch?' she said, aghast.

He looked at her bare legs and feet and the clinging silk robe and gave a grim smile. 'I don't intend to take my eyes off you, sweetheart.'

Ami walked to her spare room, conscious of him following close behind. *Sweetheart*. Perhaps he wouldn't remember her real face when he saw it. Perhaps it wasn't *her* he'd meant when he spoke of instant attractions. It was probably some other woman who'd caught his eye, the arrogant swine. The man was so damned sexist that he probably couldn't remember one woman from another.

Ami sat at her make-up mirror and watched him manhandle a chair to sit astride it, facing her over its back. He reached for the wig, studied it intently, a muscle flickering in his cheek. He slapped it a couple of times against the edge of the table.

'Be careful,' Ami protested. 'That's a very expensive item. Real European hair on the best imported lace base, and it has to go back into stock at the shop—'

She met his eyes and her protest stuck in her throat. Using tweezers, she peeled off the tissue-thin edges of the foam latex prosthetics one by one. The neck pieces, the forehead, the eye pouches all moulded to the cast of her own face. 'Latex. I make them myself,' she said nervously, for something to say, but it was clear North Kendrick was not interested in the technical process that had hoodwinked him. Coldly he regarded each piece of trickery, slapping the expensive wig against his hand from time to time, saying nothing, speaking volumes. Ami moved slowly, unwilling to be revealed to North Kendrick. It was as embarrassing as doing a striptease. She bent and smothered her face with white cleansing cream to remove the remaining bits of adhesive and stippled colour. 'In Elizabethan days,' she said, aware that time was running out as she wiped the last traces of her disguise away, 'actors used to use chunks of pig fat to remove their make-up. It's the origin of the nickname ''hams'' for actors.'

'Fascinating,' he growled.

Her face was a little pink, but back to normal. She raised her head and looked at him in the mirror. North Kendrick stiffened. The rhythmic slapping of the grey wig stopped sharply.

'What the hell—*you*!'

Ami experienced a vain satisfaction that he *had* remembered her face. Slowly she removed the ageing yellow stain from her teeth, took out the contact lenses that had clouded her aquamarine eyes. She brushed her flattened hair. It crackled with static electricity, flying out from her scalp, strands clinging to her face. He grasped her chin, jerked her around to him, and she whirled on her swivel stool. The hard, grey eyes looked into hers, blinked rapidly. His nostrils distended as he subjected her to a long, intense scrutiny.

'All colours guaranteed natural,' she said dryly.

She felt the angry flex of his fingers on her chin, the short gusts of his breath. Abruptly, he transferred his hand to the back of her chair, and the move inched the castors forward so that she was propelled closer to him.

'Just what is your game?'

'Not the one you thought it was,' she retorted.

'You're not from SOPS, I checked. Some kind of scam, then,' he said slowly, suspicion squinting his thick-lashed eyes into slits. 'A confidence trick, maybe. Now what are you after? Money, naturally, but—'

'No. The first time I saw you I was just doing a job for my mother,' she said.

He gave a snort of incredulity. 'Ah, a job on the streets for your *mother*. And what do we call her—*Madam* Winterburn?'

Ami glowered at him, thinking in other circumstances it would have been hilarious. 'I was doing some research for her agency, as it happens, but that's none of your business. You and your guards confused me with someone else,' she said shortly. 'I'd never been near your hotel until that day. I'm a make-up artist, not a confidence trickster.'

'There's a difference?' he sneered.

'I'm not interested in your money. Nor am I interested in *you*.'

'Did I say that?'

'"Without wishing to sound conceited, I can tell when a woman is interested—and she was,"' she said, mimicking his voice. 'Well, here it is, straight from the horse's mouth. She *wasn't*.'

His nostrils flared and there was a flush of colour high on his cheeks. North was still having trouble remembering that everything he'd said to harmless, grandmotherly Amelia had actually been said to Ami Winterburn. She shifted slightly, her skin prickling with the heat from the light bulbs around her make-up mirror.

'I don't believe you,' he murmured. 'I'm good at reading signals.' There was a moment when she could have run for cover but it had already passed when he leaned forward and the reflection of a dozen lights glittered in his eyes as he clamped a hand to her nape and kissed her. She made a muffled sound of outrage that he would choose this way to express his anger. And he was angry, she could feel the rage shimmering around him, feel it in the imprisoning grasp of his large hand on her neck and the fierce pressure of his mouth on hers.

Abruptly, he stopped, and Ami dragged a hand ostentatiously across her mouth. 'Yuck,' she said with great deliberation.

Unexpectedly, he laughed without making a sound. 'It was good for me.'

Her pulses clamoured. 'It was a power play, so it would be, wouldn't it?' He had not released her and she felt the flex of his hand at the nape of her neck, the merest touch of his breath on her face. Her knees touched his and she was hotly aware of the intimate contact.

'I should have known you couldn't be on the game,' he said, almost to himself. 'Because all the men you approached walked away from you again.' He paused a moment, gazing into her eyes. 'That's a compliment.'

Ami glared. 'Do you really think so?'

He looked at her mouth and touched it with his thumb, the way he had that day in the cab. Her heart hammered away in her chest, her throat felt dry.

'Shall we try it again?' he said.

'I can't think of anything I'd like less.'

'Liar. You criticised my technique. That's practically a challenge to me to do it again.'

And this time it was a different kind of power play. Not a display of strength, but one of persuasion. He moved his head slightly, from side to side, rubbing his lips across hers. Ami kept her eyes open, fiercely gazing into his to show him that his expertise was wasted. He smiled and took it as another challenge. She saw the sudden answering gleam in his eyes as his fingers slid into her hair and his mouth parted hers in a quick, confident demand. Her eyelids drooped. Kisses, in her experience, were inclined to be sloppy, disappointing things. North, she thought distractedly, was a virtuoso. Authority with gentleness, sensuality with restraint. She had wondered what it would be like to be kissed by him but the reality rocked her. His tongue dipped inside, languorously withdrew and his mouth slid across her cheek to the sensitive skin of her temple and down beneath her ear. Her hand, set against him in rejection, now curved to the shape of his arm and she felt the bulk of muscle and the texture of fine wool beneath her fingers.

'Ami Winterburn,' he said against her mouth as if he was completing his identification of her.

She inched back, mortified that she could be seduced by physical magnetism and a slick technique. Abruptly she turned her chair on its swivel, came face to face with herself in the mirror. Her cheeks were flushed, and there was a moist shine to her lips. She tore a tissue from the box and wiped the wanton look from her mouth as she met his eyes in the mirror.

'Like I said,' North murmured, a complacent smile curving his mouth. 'I rarely get it wrong.'

'You got everything wrong the *first* time you saw me,' she reminded him, tossing the used tissue into a bin and the traces of his kiss with it. 'You got everything wrong the *second* time. So maybe you've got it wrong yet again, have you thought of that?'

He looked hard at her, the way he had when he'd first seen her face with the disguise removed, as if he didn't quite trust the apparent genuineness of it. For a man who had hardly put a foot wrong in fifteen years, it must be galling to be fooled.

'I've thought a great many things tonight,' he said in a soft, biting tone. 'Most of them punishable by long sentences in maximum security jails.'

He got up and went into the hall. She looked at the wig and bit her lip. The man was awful, but she supposed she did owe him an apology to conclude this stupid business.

Ami hurried after him, catching him as he reached for the front door. 'Mr. Kendrick—North—at least let me apologise for, um, Amelia and explain how—'

She grabbed his arm and he spun around, shoving her hand off as if it was a contaminant. 'How the hell are you going to *explain* why you duped my guests, involved me in some kind of—of sick joke!'

She threw her arms out and said, 'All right! I'm sorry. It escalated into something I never intended, I admit,' she said. 'But it was your own fault, basically.'

'My fault? *My* fault that an important night of my life was dominated by a—a phoney pensioner gibbering about bloody *lamp shades*?' he roared. 'And the worst of it is—I *liked* her!'

He stood very still, hands on hips, looking at the ceiling for twenty seconds. His chest rose and fell as he took deep, calming breaths. Ami crossed her fingers that it would work. She looked around for a weapon in case it didn't. Maybe she should let Spritz inside. The dog was making a racket at the back door. She inched toward it.

'I just wanted to get into your hotel,' she said reasonably, using her most soothing voice. 'You'd thrown me out on the strength of some second-hand description, insulted me. *Banned* me, told Morgan never to let me darken your door again. So naturally I had to go inside just *once*. To restore my self-esteem.'

His eyes came down from the ceiling to fix, incredulously, on her. 'Your self-esteem.'

'I just happened to have the aged make-up on, so I thought—Morgan would never recognise me like this.' She turned her head and shouted through the door. 'Be quiet, Spritz!'

'You just *happened* to look like someone's grand-mother!'

'I'd given a special-effects demonstration to some students,' she said, slowly and carefully so as not to enrage him further. 'It takes a good ninety minutes to apply and I'd done such a good job it seemed a pity to waste it.' His mouth actually hung open for a moment. He closed it with a snap of his jaw worthy of a fresh-water crocodile and she judged that it was too late to soothe him. Frankly she went on, 'Look, I would have been into the coffee shop and out again and no-one the wiser if I hadn't been treated like a second-class citizen—yet again.'

'Don't you dare try to justify this fraud!'

'*Come home to heaven*—but not if you don't look right for the occasion. Not if you're old and don't match the furnishings and look powerless enough to just be shoved off. Morgan had the nerve to tell me to run along home and come back another time, *you* sent that young man to show me the door—'

'I did no such thing,' he snapped.

'Oh, well, then Morgan must have, so he thought he was only interpreting *your* wishes. And *you* patronised me—yet again.'

'What the hell are you talking about?' he yelled over Spritz's escalating yelps.

'"You shall have *all* the coffee you can drink,"' she mimicked, patting the nearest lounge chair in imitation of his consoling manner with Amelia.

It was the wrong thing to say on several counts. His eyes glittered and she was reminded that it was not much more than an hour since she was sitting in his office while he poured out coffee and confidences.

'You have the gall to talk about social injustice when I was photographed by the press, waltzing with an old woman who is actually twenty-six years old! *Waltzing*,' he repeated and his head went back as if he was only now collating the many separate grudges he had against her. Was he thinking of that moment when she'd slipped and ended up close in his arms?

'Well, you shouldn't have asked Amelia to dance, should you? I tried to refuse but you were just too masterful for your own good. Considering the public relations value you got from waltzing with poor old Amelia, it's churlish of you to resent it now.'

'Churlish!' he shouted. 'You unprincipled little— You let Harry innocently invite her—*you* to dinner, you accepted my hospitality, made fools of an old man and me and you dare to criticise *me*!' Spritz was going crazy in the back garden, and half the neighbourhood dogs were barking in sympathy. North strode to the back door, flung it open and bellowed, 'Be *quiet*!'

The racket stopped. He slammed the door and Ami jumped. His jaw gritted and Ami thought it highly likely that he was grinding his teeth. A continuing, obedient silence from outside enhanced her wariness. Spritz seemed hardly reliable as a secret weapon if she could be silenced so readily. It didn't seem the time to tell North that only he had been the fool, that innocent old Harry had been in on the joke all along. He would realise that soon enough.

'What can I say? I'm not sorry I did it because you drove me to it, but I *am* sorry it went so far,' she said again, her arms spread wide in apology. North Kendrick stared at her in the oddest way. 'There is no real harm done, is there? I didn't give the agency the tape-recording. It wouldn't be ethical because you gave your name and—'

'Tape-recording!' He seized her, his thumbs pressing into the soft flesh inside her elbows. She was no featherweight but the pressure lifted her forward, onto the balls of her feet and too close inside the range of his hard, grey eyes. 'What tape-recording? When? Where the hell did you plant a microphone? Who are you working for?'

'You're hurting me,' she said, wincing at the bruising strength of his hands. The pressure eased slightly, not enough. 'Look, I'm not some kind of corporate spy, if that's what you're thinking. Are all businessmen so paranoid? I thought actors were bad enough. It was in my handbag. Do you want it? The tape, I mean.'

'Well, I don't want your bloody handbag,' he said between his teeth.

Ami hurried to fetch the tape from her living room. 'You can have it. Naturally, it all ends here. You have my word that I won't tell anyone about it—my disguise, I mean, and how successful it was.'

'Your word,' he said, curling his lip.

'Yes. My word!' She slapped the tape into his hand and he took a few moments to consider it before he tucked it into his inside pocket. It cost her dearly, but Ami held out her hand to him in a staunch gesture of goodwill. Anything to make an end to this awful business. 'No hard feelings, I hope?' Too late she realised that it sounded like a mocking mimicry of his own words to her the day of the gardenia.

North looked her over as if she was an alien life form. He opened the door and stepped outside then looked back at her. His voice was very low, very controlled. 'You're the one who has it all wrong, Miss Winterburn, if you think this is where it ends.'

He closed the door behind him and she braced herself for another slam. Instead, it made a small, sinister snick. Ami listened for the sound of a car departing and it, too, was moderate, controlled. It would have made her feel less anxious had he slammed a few doors and revved his motor.

Ami phoned Emma with a much edited version of the evening's activities and made a date to see her the following evening. She fed Spritz and did some chores and failed to relax in a deep, warm bath. North Kendrick. Less like a man's name and more like an address. Where are you going? To North Kendrick.

It was unfortunate that Kendrick seemed to be associated with so many powerful sensual triggers. Smell. The heavy scent of gardenia. Hearing. The insistent sound of the waltz that echoed in her head. Touch. His kiss. She touched her lips, recalling the sensation of his mouth on hers, and her body reacted with a primitive thrill. I hardly know him, she thought, shocked. I don't *want* to know him. Ami clambered from the bath and wrapped herself tightly in a towelling robe. Just where, she wondered, *would* it all end?

CHAPTER FOUR

'WE MUST decide on Christmas decorations for the shop,' her partner said the next day when Ami had farewelled her weekly make-up students, all wearing scars and bruises of their own creation.

Ami groaned. 'Helen—September's only just finished!'

'Time slips away and the Christmas cards are already out in the supermarket,' Helen said with a hunted air. 'I've started my Christmas shopping. This year I am *not*, absolutely *not* going to get stuck with last-minute shopping.'

Ami straightened some eye-shadow palettes and fantasy eyelashes. Using the shelf as a *barre*, she performed a few ballet stretches to get out the kinks from an hour of close work bending over fake wounds and contusions. 'You're not going to insist on artificial snow on the windows this year, are you?'

'Why not?'

'It's ridiculous. Here we are, sweltering in a hot south land full of gums and palm trees and we spray fake snow on our windows and stick blobs of cotton wool on fir trees and try to make the sub-tropics look like Victorian England in winter.'

Helen looked shocked. 'But you must have a pine tree for Christmas, and snow. And stars. We always put gold stars on our front window at home for Christmas. Everyone in the street expects it.'

Ami dipped low, arching her arm down so that her fingers skimmed the floor. 'All those portly men sweating away on city streets in Santa suits. Even when I was a

53

little kid, I wondered why so many Santas sweated. He never did in story books. By the way, I've ordered in some Santa beards for Christmas.'

Helen said something she didn't hear. 'Ami,' she added, louder, to get her attention.

As she straightened, Ami saw there was a customer in the shop. She was smiling her dazzling smile of welcome before she saw who it was. The smile switched off. By daylight he looked more tanned and physical, even in the precise drape of a pin-striped double-breasted suit. Eyeing his width of shoulder, she wondered how she had ever thought he might be skinny. Pure wishful thinking, trying to cut him down to size.

'Ami,' Helen said, 'this is Mr. Kendrick. He came in earlier, about make-up for a promotion, while you were with the class. This is Ami Winterburn, our principal and genius with make-up and special effects.' Helen smiled rather archly at North Kendrick. 'Perhaps you'd like to see some of Ami's work—'

'I've already seen some of Miss Winterburn's work.' He took a long, measuring look at Ami's svelte figure in shirt, vest and black pants tucked into short boots, her streaky blonde hair twitched casually into a bunch on one side of her head. 'Genius might be an exaggeration, but I think she's quite good,' he said to Helen, keeping his eyes on Ami.

'I'm almost sure it would take a genius to fool *you*, Mr. Kendrick,' Ami said with false admiration.

His ruler-straight mouth crimped a bit at that.

'You might like to see our design samples,' Helen said, frowning at Ami's lack of enthusiasm for a prospective customer. Crouching down, Helen sorted through their photo collection of make-up designs, sliding folders onto the counter surface.

North Kendrick walked away, looking around the small space at the displays of stock. After a slight hesitation, Ami followed him. He studied a wig made en-

tirely of curled silver foil strips, took a jaundiced view
of a display board of false noses. 'What could the queen
of illusion possibly have against fake snow at Christmas?'
he said sardonically.

'I just don't like pretend snow in summer.'

'But you're ordering in Santa beards.'

Ami shrugged, flashed the palms of her hands. 'That's
business.'

He held up a bottle of artificial tears and perspiration. 'I find it contradictory—not at all what I would
expect.'

'I must be awfully complex, then,' she said with gentle
sarcasm.

He smiled. 'I see your partner doesn't know about
your escapade. Didn't she see your sweet little old face
alongside mine in the newspaper this morning?'

Guilt made Ami flush. The picture had been a large
one, of her and North, waltzing. *Gatecrashing Granny*,
the inane caption went. She had looked fantastic—old
enough to be his mother. Her thrill of professional pride
had only lasted until Emma phoned her to ask her if she
was out of her mind and to offer the name of a very
good lawyer. 'I haven't told Helen yet. But if that's what
it takes to satisfy you, go ahead and tell her yourself.'

Turning a small pot in his hand, he glanced at her,
said ambiguously, 'That isn't what it will take to satisfy
me.'

Ami snorted. 'Am I supposed to be thrown into maidenly confusion by that?'

'Are you ever thrown into maidenly confusion?'

By him she was, she thought, but he would be the last
to know it.

He held up the tiny pot. 'What's this?'

'Congealed blood,' she said feelingly.

He put it down, lifted a make-up palette and viewed
the assortment of yellows, greens and purples. 'And
you'd use these colours for?'

'Bruises,' she said, picking out a perfect site for one on the arrogant line of his jaw.

His eyes went to a realistic bruise on her wrist, where she'd demonstrated for her students. 'More of your work?' he asked, looking at it with genuine interest. Ami was tempted to say that she had some real bruises just emerging, from his brutish handling the night before. 'Very realistic. I want to talk to you. Come to the hotel tomorrow.'

A command, not an invitation. 'Tomorrow? Thursday?' she said in dismay.

'One-thirty sharp. Come as yourself—if you know what that is. The widow Anderson is not required.'

'I'm tied up with a make-up class tomorrow. I can't be back by one-thirty.'

'More lessons in illusion?' he said derisively. 'Teaching others how to appear what they aren't? Cancel it.'

She was tempted. If he only knew, every week she wished for a legitimate reason to cancel this particular class. And that was why she never did. 'Absolutely not.'

He studied her with such care that Ami wondered when someone had last said no to him. 'You know I could ruin you if I chose to?' he said softly.

Her heart gave a bump. Ruin? In their current state of business, that wouldn't take much doing. With his resources he could buy the building, put up their rent. That alone would be enough to finish them off. Guardedly, Ami met his eyes. 'I suppose you could,' she said, picturing herself and Helen as the puny target of a multimillion-dollar enterprise. 'I can make it by two-thirty. If I don't arrive on time, then you've still got all afternoon to ruin me.'

He laughed, the sudden flash of teeth taking her by surprise. 'All right, two-thirty.' North inclined his head by way of concession but Ami had a feeling that she had just been outmanouvred by an expert. While she'd been busy asserting herself over *which* time, she had quite forgotten that she should have refused to go at all. She tried to disguise a moue of vexation.

Smiling, he thrust the palette into her hand. 'Your bruises, Miss Winterburn.'

The door closed behind him. Ami let out a deep breath. Helen had followed the final folder upwards and leaned on the desk, dismayed at the customer who'd got away.

'Ami, what's going on? Why were you so *aggressive* with the man? He was the *good* news!'

Ami laughed so much that in the end she had to explain to Helen why North Kendrick couldn't be considered good news. 'His talk about a make-up job was just a ploy to take a closer look at the shop, have a sniff around. The man isn't going to let me get away with making a fool of him.'

Dazed by Ami's quick-fire confession about her disguise, she said, 'Are you sure he didn't guess? He looks too shrewd to be fooled by anything or anyone.'

'About money, maybe, about numbers and percentages, but Mr. Kendrick isn't so hot when it comes to people.' She paused, thinking of the fragile state of North's relationship with his father, wondered why she felt so sad about it when he hardly deserved sympathy.

'And the press took photographs?'

Ami squirmed. She braced herself for recriminations, for a perfectly justified bawling out by her partner, for juvenile behaviour. But when Helen had been shown the newspaper photo and assimilated the story, what she said was, 'What was he like to dance with?'

Ami went to the hotel the next day at two-thirty. Let him call the shots and waste her time if it made him feel better. He was entitled to his anger, she admitted grudgingly. She kept her sunglasses on as she entered and overrode her depressed Thursday mood with some semblance of breeziness for the sake of pride.

Morgan was on the door. He looked swiftly over her black pants, baggy lilac cotton sweater, short boots and three inches of silver bangles and gave her a sheepish smile to show that his instructions had been reversed since the day of the gardenia.

'Never forget a face, Mr. Morgan? Or should I say, a face or two?' she added, unable to resist reminding him that she'd got past him in her disguise.

The doorman looked blankly at her and Ami realised he didn't know that she and the old lady who had caused a fuss were one and the same.

'Mr. Kendrick will be down in a moment, Miss Winterburn.'

She sat down and felt very ill-used when he kept her waiting fifteen minutes. He arrived at last, not a hair out of place, not a pucker on his charcoal suit jacket. Silk tie and matching pocket handkerchief. It was an intimidating picture he made, the handsome, successful man, striding across his marble floor with his vast hotel foyer as a backdrop, staff members all but tugging their forelocks and women guests ogling him.

'You haven't told Morgan about my stint as the widow,' she said breezily, to deny the feeling of intimidation.

'Not yet. You can apologise to Morgan another time. Right now you have a more important apology to make.'

She frowned over this as they entered his private lift. 'I've already apologised but if you want me to grovel, let me do it now to save time.'

He didn't answer, just silently reviewed her appearance and when the lift opened on his foyer, took her elbow to urge her into the lake-and-island living room.

'You can grovel to me later. I thought we'd have lunch and preliminary grovelling first—with Harry.'

'Harry?' she said, faltering at the steely, significant look he bestowed on her.

'He was asleep when I returned last night so I haven't told him yet, either. *You* can have that pleasure,' he said.

Ami's eyes opened wide. 'Oh, but—I mean, Harry—'

He misread her dismay, gave a sardonic smile. 'I'm glad to see even you have some conscience. I'll be most interested to see how you tell my father that the widow Anderson is a fraud.' He gestured ahead to the terrace where Harry sat in his wheelchair, studying the city through a pair of binoculars. Ami looked at Harry, licked her lips and once again he mistook the reason for her dismay. She'd thought by now that Harry would have been gloating about the deception. Surely, when North had reflected on it he would have *guessed* Harry knew? Taking in his glacial smile of satisfaction, she felt a sudden shaft of pity. Clever, shrewd, arrogant North Kendrick hadn't even considered that his father was in on the joke. It was an appealing blind spot in such a clever man. But she felt terrible, privy to a humiliating knowledge. Impulsively, she grabbed his sleeve, held back his relentless forward progress. 'Look, I don't think you—could you stop for a minute—*North*!' She dragged on his arm and he stopped suddenly, sliding an arm around her waist to steady them both.

'*Ami*!' he said, mocking her urgent tone. His breath swept across her cheek, and his arm tightened around her in extravagant, loverlike fashion. 'Didn't you say that's what your friends call you?' he said in her ear, as if it was an endearment rather than a rhetorical question.

Ami was disconcerted, shaken by the heat generated by his voice and the touch of his arm hard around her. *I was attracted to her...* She pulled back, aware of a tiny flare of triumph that the attraction was still active, feeling the force of the earthy nature of it. Her heart thumped, her breath seemed strangled in her throat. It was some kind of chemistry but surely she was only receptive to it because she was in her emotional Thursday afternoon state.

'You asked me what would satisfy me,' he murmured, stroking an index finger down her hair. 'Now you know.'

Her silver bracelets jangled as she batted his hand away and glared at him. He laughed, lifted her sunglasses off and regarded her quizzically. 'Red eyes. Tch, tch, have I made you cry, Ami?'

Taking back the glasses, Ami said, 'I only cry about important things. I've just been demonstrating for students again.'

'It's a very subtle effect,' he said, frowning.

'Of course. All my work is very good. That's why I'm here, isn't it?' she mocked.

'Are all make-up girls so conceited?'

'Are all chief executives so patronising?'

He looked enquiringly at her.

'If I were twenty-six and male, would you refer to me as a make-up *boy*?' she said, warming to her theme. 'I am a make-up *artist*. I am not a girl. I am a *woman*.'

'I hear you roar,' he said blandly.

Taking her elbow again, he marched her toward the terrace. A small table was set to look like a cookery-book lunch illustration. Starched napkins, a basket of crusty bread rolls, a glass-domed cheese platter. Green and purple grapes in a high-stemmed goblet. Chilled glasses and a bottle of wine in an ice bucket. Even Kendrick's lunch looked like a work of art.

Harry lowered his binoculars and in just a moment would look their way. 'North, I'm trying to tell you that, um, Harry, well, Harry—' She licked her lips and rushed to finish as the old man turned his wheelchair. 'Harry already knows.'

North stopped dead, looked at Harry and his eyes flew open wide as if someone had clashed cymbals in his ear. For a moment he looked as oddly vulnerable as he had in that photo of him as a boy. Ami felt a rush of tenderness for him, an astonishing wish to put her arms around the arrogant, complacent man.

The wheelchair came humming over. Harry inspected Ami from head to toe with intense appreciation. A wheezing laugh broke from him. 'I *said* you'd be a good-looking woman under those wrinkles, didn't I?'

Beside her North stiffened. Harry guffawed and took a white handkerchief from his pocket to wipe his eyes. Ami stood miserably in the drawn-out silence broken only by Harry's wheezing laughter and the muffled sound of city traffic below.

'And what made you think she wasn't what she seemed?' North said harshly.

'It was her joints that gave her away.'

'Joints?' North Kendrick said, biting down on the word as if it was indeed a bone. A flush of colour appeared high on the younger man's cheeks. His jaw clenched so hard, a muscle twitched in his cheek. 'And the birthday dinner? That was cooked up between you?' he said, grinding out the pun. 'All that cosy chitchat about my misdemeanors as a kid, the baby photographs, the double entendres...' His voice rose and cut off abruptly before he said to Ami, 'You even had me rambling on about how you reminded me of my grandmother.'

'Oh, I know that's unforgivable,' she said, distressed. 'And quite unintended. I felt a terrible cheat—'

'That's because you *are* a cheat.'

'You weren't supposed ever to know,' she said, colour surging into her face. 'It was just a joke Harry was going to enjoy privately.' North's nostrils flared and she was reminded that it was only a short time ago that she was telling him about her own private joke that had gone wrong. 'If it hadn't been for that purse snatcher you never *would* have known. Amelia would have disappeared and you none the wiser.'

The idea of being none the wiser seemed to have no appeal for him, either. 'And did it entertain you?' he asked, in a low, dangerous voice that sent shivers down her spine. Harry went off into paroxysms again.

'Is all this sniggering good for you, Harry?' North bit out.

'Oh, come on, boy. Where's your sense of humour? You seem to have lost it since you've become so high and mighty. You always were a bit too serious for your own good but you're getting to be a real stuffed shirt these days.'

Genuine amazement broke up the ice on North's face. 'A stuffed shirt?' He seemed startled, even hurt by the criticism but recovered quickly. 'I don't appreciate you conniving with a total stranger and raking over private family matters with her. How dare you abuse my privacy by inviting a conscienceless, malicious fraud into my home to ridicule me!' His voice had risen to a shout. In awful fascination, Ami saw that his control was almost broken. Anger tensed every line of his body. The flickering muscle in his cheek quickened. He made a rageful sweep with one fist and she winced, half expecting the still-life lunch to go flying.

'Yeah, well, I'm not too thrilled, either,' Harry said in a tone quite different from his usual geniality. It was surprisingly like his son's. 'You know why you're in such a temper? Because you can't believe your dumb old man could work something out that fooled *you*, the genius!'

Once again North was visibly affected by the attack from his father, and Ami wished passionately that she wasn't here to witness it. He already held so many grudges against her. After a moment he turned away.

'That's right—just turn your back on me. It doesn't matter what I think, does it?' Harry roared. 'I'm just a sick old man you picked up from the hospital because you thought it was your duty.'

'That's enough, Harry,' North said through gritted teeth. 'I don't intend to discuss private matters in front of this—' His jaw worked as he searched without success for a word to describe her. 'As for you, Miss Winterburn—you have ten minutes to say your goodbyes and be out on the street.'

Where you belong. The unspoken phrase resounded. Thrown out again. Ami turned scarlet.

'If my friends aren't welcome here, I won't be staying, either,' Harry bellowed as North strode away. This time North didn't stop. He disappeared inside, until his progress was a mere movement behind the walls of glass that reflected towers and shifting cloud. Ami couldn't stand the man, but she wouldn't wish the situation on her worst enemy. Sympathy for him warred with her fury at his high-handed, insulting manner. She was angry with both of them, sad for both of them. Her own family life might be chaotic at times but never like this. There was a solid affection that underpinned her relationship with her parents, and this stormy exchange left her feeling shaky and battered.

The old man said gruffly, 'Stay a minute, have a grape.' He offered her the fruit then held out the binoculars to her and it wouldn't have made her stay except that his hand trembled. She took the glasses and looked where he directed, at a building he had worked on in his youth. 'The old Century Hotel. I did a nice bit of panelling in the dining room. Wonder if it's still there?' he said to himself. 'I thought, if I let him bring me here after the operation, we'd maybe work out how to get along together at last, North and me,' he said sadly. 'But I suppose it's too late for that now.'

When she left, he wheeled alongside her to the elevator, gave her a slip of paper with his address and phone number on it. 'Come and see me when I'm back in my own place, Ami.'

She kissed his cheek, thinking it was unlikely she would visit Harry. Where Harry was, North might be and it was a risk she would rather not take. The sooner she got the Kendrick men out of her life, the better.

A week passed without a sign of North Kendrick. CKC was finalising the purchase of a well-known electronics chain and business writers were hinting that North Kendrick would soon turn his attention to buying into the media. Shrewd, clever, realistic, a consummate player, they called him. Yet shrewd, clever North Kendrick had displayed a naive faith in his father's loyalty, had even been outraged on his father's behalf when he thought Ami had deceived Harry, too. There was nothing so savage as righteous outrage discovered to be unnecessary. Nothing so humiliating as blind faith shattered. After such a colossal loss of face North Kendrick probably wouldn't seek her out again, even for revenge. It was a cause for celebration that left her feeling curiously flat.

'Ami, dear, I've got a job that's right up your street— walking two Borzoi dogs one hour a day. It needs someone who can sing.'

'Sing? Why?'

'The dogs like to be sung to during their walk. The owner's lost her voice. I thought of you at once, you sing so nicely.'

'Mother—' Ami groaned into the phone, turning over in bed to peer at her clock. It was barely seven on Friday morning. 'No—not another job that's right up my street. Please take my name off your books.'

'Ami, my love, you must know that a daughter's name will always be on a mother's books,' her mother said affectionately. 'But all right, if you don't want the Borzoi job, I won't hound you,' she went on with her un-faltering flair for words. 'Don't forget the art exhibition tonight. It's a marvellous nineteenth-century private collection, I understand, and this is the only chance to see it in Sydney. The owner's grown tired of it and is donating it to a gallery in Melbourne, I believe. Pre-Raphaelite, art nouveau—I've got your ticket. Do come. We're trying to persuade the collector to donate a work of art to us for a fundraiser, and a good turn-up would make a strong argument.'

Ami wrinkled her nose. 'I hate nineteenth-century art. All those listless women with peekaboo breasts and red hair, languishing over bowls of fruit and sheafs of wheat.'

'That's all right, dear. It's *art*. You don't have to like it.'

But, in fact, Ami had to admit even if she didn't like the style it was a fine collection, shown to curious advantage in a modern house that occupied several levels on a steep, rocky site overlooking Pittwater. A solo violinist played to the viewers of paintings, posters, sculptures, lamps, glassware, all of which incorporated dragons, deities, anguished maidens, voluminous robes and lilies. There was even a fountain, fully operational and mossy in a sheltered courtyard, spouting water from the open mouths of several fish that clustered around a brace of underdressed women. Looking at the eight ripe, bare breasts pointing in an angle identical to that of the fishes, Ami thought it was a mercy that the water was gushing where it was.

'Wonderful, isn't it?' Lenore Winterburn said to her.

'Hideous, but beautifully executed,' she allowed. Ami stopped abruptly to eye a row of sculpted nymphs that wouldn't look out of place outside the Avalon. She could almost imagine North Kendrick alongside one of them, a hand proprietarially on a perfect white marble thigh. 'Does this owner have any furniture other than collector's items?' Ami asked, looking around at the open spaces between exhibits.

'He doesn't live here anymore, actually. Too many stairs for him now, Erica said, so I suppose the poor man must have trouble with his mobility. There's just his collection and the security people here, which is why he agreed to the exhibition, because it doesn't interfere with his privacy anymore. I believe the house is to be rented out soon, and the collection will all be packed up and sent to Melbourne.' She looked speculatively at the quartet of garlanded female figures. 'I wonder if he would give the society one of those nymphs to raffle.'

Ami laughed. 'You can't raffle a nymph. It's disrespectful.'

But her mother had turned to look behind her for the committee president who was doing the rounds with various charity VIPs, making introductions. 'I suppose that must be the owner with Erica—the one in the wheelchair,' Lenore murmured in Ami's ear.

'Wheelchair?' Ami said, feeling a prickling sensation between her shoulder-blades. She turned. North Kendrick was behind her, no more than a nymph away.

CHAPTER FIVE

HER pulse, grown sluggish at the prospect of yet more sculptures and small talk with her mother's charity committee friends, raced into a hectic rhythm. He was in profile by a sculpture giving its provenance to three very attentive women. As they made comments, he bent his dark head and nodded. He placed a hand on the sculptured knee of a nymph and Ami heard him say, 'Exquisite.'

As if her gaze had alerted him, he turned his head. He didn't recognise her instantly, probably because it was the last place he expected to see her. Also probably because she had made a concession to her mother's favourite charity and dressed in an elegant, thin-strapped dress of caramel silk and oiled back her long hair into a classic dancer's knot. A delicate, beaded plait hung each side of her face. Her skirt was above the knee and her long legs looked longer still in high heels, a fact that Kendrick appeared to be noting. His hand withdrew from the nymph's white thigh when he realised whose legs he was admiring. A thunderous look transformed him, to the dismay of the charity committee, for whom all had been going so well.

He excused himself and walked forward. 'Miss Winterburn, we meet yet again.'

She smiled with a great deal more composure than she felt as he eyed her intently. 'Mr. Kendrick.'

'What do you think of the show?'

'The violinist is very good,' she said earnestly.

A sardonic smile tilted his mouth. He raked another look over her sleek, oil-darkened hair, her bare shoulders

67

and the hint of cleavage showing at her neckline. 'Disguised again? Do you ever look the same twice?'

Ami determined to keep her temper. Her mother, summoned away by the committee president, would never forgive her if she made a scene with the committee's benevolent art collector.

'Harry's with you, I see,' she said, looking hopefully in Harry's direction, but he hadn't seen her yet.

North's eyes narrowed. 'Yes, he is, no thanks to you.'

She bit her lip to hold back a sharp retort, resentful that he should try to blame her for widening a rift in a relationship that was already in trouble. 'This is your collection then?' she went on doggedly. 'I didn't know.'

'Really? You keep turning up in my life, Miss Winterburn. You can't expect me to believe it's sheer coincidence. What are you doing here?'

Ami's good intentions slipped away. 'Oh, I'm casing the joint,' she mocked. 'I thought I might nick a nymph or two.'

His mouth smiled but his eyes remained cool and watchful. He glanced around quickly, as if searching for conspirators.

'I'm working alone again,' she drawled, reminding him of previous errors of judgement.

'You're good value, I'll give you that,' he said, laughing. 'Come with me.'

He took her arm and walked her through the scattered crowd and she could hardly make a fuss without ruining the occasion. Everyone took an interest. Ami raised a hand to Harry, who waved cheerfully at her and, to her chagrin, didn't even attempt to come after her. And her mother, who never hesitated to butt in where she wasn't wanted, now failed to butt in exactly where she *was* wanted.

Red-faced, she said, 'Where are you taking me? Going to hand me over to your gung-ho security officers for interrogation?'

'Why should they have all the fun?' He guided her into a room mercifully free of the whiplash curves of art nouveau. It was furnished with a large, plain desk, a couple of chairs and a drinks cabinet. A green-shaded table lamp was switched on, illuminating some paperwork. He went to the drinks cabinet, took out two glasses and a bottle of champagne from an ice bucket. He poured the wine, came back to hand her a glass.

'This is a very civilised interrogation,' she said lightly, taking a sip. He drank from his glass, watching her as he did so, and a silence stretched out in the room. The collective hum of voices wafted through from the exhibition. Down the rocky slope, trees shushed in the salt breeze, the sound a mimesis of that other rhythmic rush of water on sand below. The violin played an English folk song, a descant over the mellow murmurings.

Ami grew uneasy. His hard-eyed look reminded her that she had been privy to his humiliation on Thursday. 'I am sorry about Thursday,' she said sincerely. 'If I'd realised earlier that you didn't know that Harry knew— I could have saved you the, er, embarrassment.'

His jaw hardened and his head went back to an arrogant angle. 'Don't patronise me, Miss Winterburn. And don't make the mistake of thinking I'm any kind of fool just because you and my father pulled a fast one on me.'

'I don't think that makes you a fool at all,' she said, shrugging. 'I think it's rather sweet and trusting that it didn't occur to you that your father would engineer a joke at your expense.'

'*Sweet?*' he said, choking on a mouthful of good, dry champagne as if it was pure saccharine. 'Good God, I think I'd prefer you thought me a fool.'

'Well, whatever you prefer, North,' she said demurely.

He laughed silently, finding her good value again, she supposed. One day, she thought maliciously, watching his shoulders heave, he would probably have one of those awful, wheezy laughs like Harry.

'Now—tell me what's going on,' he said.

'Going on? Where?'

'I wasn't born yesterday, Ami. You hang about outside my hotel, you turn up a couple of weeks later in disguise and insinuate your way into a private function, then into my private quarters. Now you turn up again at my former home. If it isn't some con game you're playing, what the hell is it?'

'Insinuate? I've told you how that happened. There is no game, do you understand? My mother invited me here tonight—'

'Ah, your *mother* again! Your inventiveness is growing threadbare.'

Ami eyed him with dislike. 'Look, think what you like. I didn't want to come here, even when I didn't know it was your place. I am not fond of the pre-Raphaelites or art nouveau, but it was for a deserving charity and I promised my mother.'

'Ami Winterburn, philanthropist, dutiful daughter,' he marvelled. 'Widow, grandmother, cheat. My God, when I said you were the kind of girl Harry wouldn't like me to take home to dinner, I might not have got it quite right but I wasn't wrong, either.'

Ami compressed her mouth. 'What's bugging you is that it was *Harry* who asked me to dinner.'

The shaft went home. His eyes glittered. 'Yes, that does bug me,' he said softly. 'But I can live with it. The question is, what am I going to do about you?'

Ami backed up a step, suddenly apprehensive so far from the crowd. Common sense told her that it was unlikely North Kendrick would do anything violent with a houseful of guests just a scream away. Ami took another step back.

'It's happened before,' he told her.

'What has?'

'A woman, turning up at odd times again and again when I least expected it. It went on for months.'

'That's the price you pay for being so irresistible,' she snapped. 'Such a bore—wait a minute! Are you implying that I am—that I am *chasing* you like this other poor, misguided woman?'

'You fit the profile. Attention-seeking behaviour, tape-recorders and disguises, insinuating your way into my private life, coming to functions I'll be attending. You make a career of fooling people,' he said thoughtfully.

'I don't fit any profile, you pompous, conceited oaf.'

'I could be wrong,' he admitted, coming toward her.

'You are.' She backed off again, then turned and strode out as best she could in high heels on the thick carpet. Heeding a warning crack in her weaker ankle, she stopped and took off her shoes. North regarded with some wariness the two metal-tipped spiked heels pointing at him.

He put his hands up in mock surrender. 'I'm unarmed.'

Ami eyed him dispassionately. 'Men like you are never unarmed.'

'Disarmed, then.' He smiled. 'If I'm suspicious it's because I never know what to make of you. I'm forced to consider the wildest possibilities.'

Her heart thumped. He stood there with a stripe of light just missing his eyes, casting a glitter in them.

'That bag snatcher might not have been unarmed,' he said softly. 'Did you think of that when you chased him?'

'It always crosses a woman's mind, I suppose, but I was so furious that he would attack an old lady I just—' She lifted one shoulder. 'He could easily have broken an arm on an elderly woman with arthritis, or osteoporosis.'

'But you weren't an elderly woman with arthritis,' he said in a curious tone.

'What's that got to do with it?' she asked, throwing her arms out. '*He* didn't know that, little creep.'

'He might be a reformed little creep now. That high kick really connected.'

'Yes, it did, didn't it?' she said with ghoulish satisfaction.

'Ballet lessons?' he enquired.

'Since I was four.'

They walked to the next doorway.

'Were you any good?'

'Yes,' she said without false modesty. 'My ambition was to join a classical ballet company but it is very competitive and I grew too tall and acquired a weak ankle, so—' She shrugged.

'And what does a failed ballet dancer do?'

Irritated at the phrase, she said airily, 'Oh—teach, join a modern dance company or do cabaret. Or,' she added with a glint in her eye, 'become an exotic dancer.'

'And which did *you* do?'

'What do you think?'

'Like I said—I always consider wild possibilities where you're concerned.'

'Are you actually entertaining ideas of me stripping in some sleazy nightclub?' she challenged, a hand on her hip.

'Mm. I, er, hadn't got as far as the sleazy nightclub,' he murmured, slanting her a look that said exactly how far he had got.

Ami mistimed her next step to the doorway and collided with North as he leaned past her to nudge the partly closed door aside. She jerked away but the doorframe was directly behind her and brought her up with a jolt no farther from him than before. The room had the chill of emptiness and she felt the radiation of heat from North's body on her shoulders and through the thin dress. He laid his hand on her bare arm and she shivered with the warmth of it.

'North—'

'Ami,' he said in the mocking way he'd said it the other day. And he bent and put his mouth to her bare shoulder, nudging aside a silk shoestring strap with his fingertips. She drew in a sharp breath and he straightened to look at the effect he'd had on her. Whatever he saw pleased him.

'I want to go back to your awful nymphs,' she said huskily.

'I'm not stopping you,' he said, breathing the words on her temple. 'But I wish you'd stay.'

He waited a moment, perhaps to give her time to leave, and when she didn't, his eyes glinted in triumph and he bent again, kissed her neck below her ear, nuzzled in so that the tiny plait swayed, its beads making small clinking noises that seemed somehow linked with the soft sounds of North's lips on her skin. The fabric of his jacket brushed against her bare skin, pleasantly abrasive. The smell of him, citron and champagne, rose in her nostrils and she reached out with her free hand to his hair. Thick, springy hair. Her fingers pushed through it, urgently. North made a throaty sound and put his hands to her waist, lifted her clear of the doorway and set her down, hauling her close against him. Her breath escaped in a startled sigh. Her hands slid beneath his jacket until her arms were around him and she felt the heat of his skin through the fine fabric of his shirt. North tilted his head and looked blazingly at her for a few seconds and she was already rising on her toes towards him when he kissed her. Her lips parted beneath his persuasive, fleeting caresses. She pressed close to him, craving more, wanting the teasing, nomadic touch to settle and deepen. She turned her head so that she captured his wandering mouth with her own, kissing him wildly, excitement trembling in her body. It had never been like this. She heard her own breathy sigh just a moment before the other voice.

'Ami, dear, where are you?'

It was her mother, butting in where she wasn't wanted.

Ami bolted from North's arms, looping her strap, smoothing her dress with trembling fingers as she amended the traitorous thought. It was her mother, butting in exactly where she was wanted for once. Ami ran her tongue over her lips. Out of the corner of her eye, she saw North quickly smooth his hair that she had ruffled so passionately. Was she crazy? She knew what kind of game he was playing, but she didn't have to make it easy for him. Lenore cast a thoughtful look over her daughter's stockinged feet, the shoes tucked under one arm, the flush on her cheeks. Then she turned her attention to North. Ami cursed silently as she saw the gleam in her mother's eyes.

'Well, I know he's not a kissing cousin,' Lenore said, removing any doubts that she might have arrived too late to see them in a clinch. 'Introduce me, Ami, my love.'

'Mum, meet North Kendrick. My mother, Lenore Winterburn.'

At least that appeared to shake him—the mythical mother so close at hand and so obviously genuine. Only a mother had such immaculate timing.

'*Madam* Winterburn,' Ami added dryly in an undertone.

Colour appeared high on his cheekbones as he courteously shook her mother's hand and weathered a scrutiny almost as thorough as any he had given Ami. North put a hand to his tie and flexed his neck. Even his superb self-confidence was rocked by the prospect of maternal criticism. Not, she noted sourly, that her mother appeared to be finding much to criticise.

'North is the owner of the collection—all those wonderful nymphs that he's grown tired of,' she said with sly malice. It would serve Mr. North Kendrick right, to get the third degree from her mother, a veritable tigress when it came to raising money for disadvantaged children. Ami put on her shoes and beat a hasty retreat from the empty rooms where she almost fancied the echo of her own sigh of pleasure hung on the air for everyone to hear.

As it happened, Lenore Winterburn spent a good twenty minutes with North, during which time even Francesca, stunning in black and silver mesh, had to take a back seat. Every now and then, North looked thoughtfully in Ami's direction and she couldn't help feeling that the donation of a nymph was not the only subject under discussion.

Her mother looked mightily pleased with herself when she rejoined Ami. 'What a charming man,' she said. 'And so modest. He makes nothing of the fact that he was a boy genius.'

'Oh, was he?' Ami said flatly, eyeing the boy genius. He was strikingly handsome in a light grey double-breasted suit of finest wool. A wolf in sheep's clothing.

'Erica told me. He was a prodigy—was inventing things when he was only fifteen and one of his schoolmasters fortunately had the wit to take out patents for him. He won all sorts of scholarships and went into high school and university years ahead of his peers, because he was so clever.'

That must have been what he meant, Ami decided, when he'd said he was always ahead of his contemporaries. *Out of step.* She pondered the significance of a boyhood spent, not with other kids his own age, but in the company of older people. Instead of carefree years at primary school, he went early into high school. When his peers were messing about in high school musicals and sneaking into nightclubs with falsified IDs, he was already at university. And the boy genius might very well have been intellectually mature, but there was every chance he had been emotionally still a little kid. It occurred to Ami that being intellectually advanced might have been a lonely business.

'Yes, he was brilliant at mathematics and science,' her mother was saying, 'and once he got into finance, he was brilliant at that, too.'

'Mathematics and science,' Ami said dryly, looking around at the languishing maidens, dragons and arum lily motifs. 'That explains a lot.'

Harry sought her out eventually. He seemed out of sorts, saying that he'd only come tonight to get away from the hotel prison. 'I don't know why he moved there. To be in the limelight when the hotel opened, I suppose,' he said pettishly.

Ami frowned at his tone. 'Isn't that a bit ungrateful, Harry? From what I can gather, North moved out of this place because all the levels and stairs were going to be a problem for you while you recovered from your op. This is a lovely house with a fabulous view. I don't suppose he particularly wanted to leave it. At least at the hotel, he can be near you with an office in the same building, and you have to admit it is easier for you with the lifts and staff when he's away.'

Harry cast her a look of such cunning that she wondered if she'd missed something. But it was gone in an instant and he was asking if she would drive him back to the hotel. 'North's going to be here for a while and I'm a bit weary.'

'I don't think your son would like that.'

'He'll like it. Let him and Francesca have some time alone—they might want to stop off somewhere and park, eh?' A suggestive wink went with this.

'Don't you think they're too old for hanky-panky in the back seat of a car?' she snapped, with a mental image of Francesca and North straightening their clothes, smoothing ruffled hair. Her cheeks burned.

'Never too old,' the old man said, giving his wheezy laugh.

'Anyway, I got the impression you weren't in favour of a match between North and Francesca,' she went on spikily.

'North's ready to settle down, I can read the signs. I'm starting to think I might have to face the inevitable,' Harry said with a sigh and a sharp look at her.

Inevitable. Ami glanced at the two prospective partners, wondering if the merger was to go ahead after all. She thought again of North, kissing her in his empty house tonight, and her temper flared. What kind of man could contemplate a union of marriage with one woman while fancying another? A collector, that's who, she thought, her eyes ranging over the exhibits. She had the panicky feeling that she must not stand still or she might join the row of nymphs. She had a vision of herself, cast in bronze standing on a plinth in a frozen pose, with North's hand possessively on her thigh.

'Well, all right then. I'll drive you,' she said to Harry. At his request, Ami dropped Harry in the hotel car park rather than the front concourse. She unfolded the wheelchair, helped him into it and, at Harry's insistence, left him waiting by the elevator. She waved, wondering if she would see him again. The idea of losing touch dismayed her. But, unless she could be certain North Kendrick was safely out of the country, she wouldn't be calling on his father.

He wasn't out of the country the next day when Ami jogged back from a run to the park with Spritz. She saw a large, pale car parked near her house, its outline fuzzed by sunshine. The footpath was a long strait ahead of her, patched with bright strips of sun and the lacy shade of arching cotoneaster branches. Ami leaped in the air to touch a branch and Spritz yelped and leaped with her as they covered the last few yards to the front gate. Laughing, exhilarated by the exercise, Ami spun into a high pirouette, taking with her the blurred impression of a man leaning on the car. She was in the air when some intuition told her who it was.

Panting, heart pounding, feet firmly on the ground, she adjusted her damp headband and stared at him.

'Very carefree,' he said sardonically, eyeing her track shoes, gym shorts and sweatshirt. 'Ami Winterburn, fitness enthusiast.' He announced it as if it was another role she was playing, another disguise she was wearing.

He didn't look carefree at all but baggy-eyed and bad-tempered and raffishly unshaven. He wore jeans and a light cotton sweater that called attention to his shoulders. His arms were crossed and the fingers of one hand tapped out a fast rhythm on his biceps. Spritz failed to absorb these antisocial signals and leaped up to lick his hand as if he was a long-lost friend instead of the barbarian who had bellowed at her on Tuesday night.

'Marvellous! My life's in chaos and you're frolicking with the dog.'

'I always frolic with the dog on Saturday,' she said. 'What's the matter? One of your languishing redheads gone missing? Lost a dryad?' She opened her eyes wide. 'You've decided art theft is the reason I *insinuated* myself into your life.'

'Always so chirpy. Doesn't it bother you that I could turn nasty and lay charges against you?' he said, and there was less threat than curiosity in the gaze that settled on her.

Ami grinned. 'Turn *nasty*? *You*?'

'It's been known,' he said without shame.

'I'm sure. Anyway, what charges could you bring against me?'

'Let's see.' He straightened and slotted his hands into his back jeans pockets, a strategy that added un-necessary inches to his shoulder span. 'Fraud? False pretences? I'd have to put it before my lawyers.'

She laughed. 'You wouldn't. You'd look ridiculous.'

North looked at the sky to compose a news item. 'Hotel magnate sues theatrical artist for false pretences. In court today, failed actress, dancer and make-up artist, Ms. Ami Winterburn, pleaded guilty to charges of false pretences—'

'You'd have to admit that Kendrick the infallible was totally taken in by a mere make-up *girl*,' she pointed out. 'Wouldn't that send share prices in CKC plummeting?'

'Hotel magnate sues theatrical company, Illusion, for false pretences. In court today, peruke maker, failed dancer and failed actress Ami Winterburn and her partner, Helen—'

Ami waved her hands urgently. 'This has nothing to do with Helen or the shop.'

'—answered charges that they practiced a malicious hoax on Connaught Kendrick, as a publicity stunt for their enterpise.'

'That's not true and you know it!'

He shrugged. 'That doesn't matter. Everyone could believe you show-biz types will do anything for publicity.'

'It's only your ego that's hurt. I truly don't believe you'd be so petty.'

'Men fight wars for their ego,' he said dryly. 'Why don't we talk inside?'

He shoved the garden gate open and waved her through, trying to establish his dominance on her own territory. And as if he needed any help, Spritz leaped alongside him and licked his hand.

'Sycophant,' she muttered. 'Heel, Spritz.'

Instead, Spritz rushed ahead, up the front patio stairs, to fetch a gnawed tennis ball in her jaws.

'Good boy,' North said, crouching as the dog brought the ball to him.

'It's a she. A good girl,' Ami said dryly. He tossed the ball and Spritz galloped to bring it back and lay it at his feet with a slavish look. 'I'll have to take her back to obedience school for a refresher course. She thinks just *anyone* is a friend.'

He slanted a look upwards at her, his eyes crinkled against the sun. 'They say animals and children can always tell. Do you think that's true?'

'I don't know. What are you like with children?'

'They dote on me.'

'Oh, really?' she said sceptically. 'Which children are these?'

'Three nieces, a nephew and two step-nephews in Melbourne. I'm godfather to two of them and to four other kids besides.'

'Six godchildren?' she said, surprised, trying to imagine him holding a baby at a christening font. Unclipping her jogger's drink bottle from her shorts waistband, Ami adjusted the plastic straw and took a cooling draught of water.

'Married people always try to find some role for their single friends—best man at the wedding, godfather at the christening, Santa Claus at Christmas. You must have experienced the same thing.'

She spluttered a little on the drink, failing miserably to imagine him in a Santa beard and red suit. 'I'm generally thought to be too tall to be in people's wedding photos.'

'Never the bridesmaid?' he quipped.

'Oh, yes, once, years ago. And I'm to be bridesmaid again soon for the same friend. Her second marriage. Emma's the same height as me,' she said in explanation, smiling at the thought of Emma's wedding.

He reviewed her height consideringly from his kneeling position. 'Two of you,' he said and gave a low whistle. 'I hope the groom is the assertive type. He might disappear without a trace.'

Ami gave a gurgle of laughter at the thought of the bearlike Mackenzie sinking without a trace. 'No, no.

Matt's a lot like you—people might hate him, or love him, but they'll never overlook him.'

'And which is it you feel for me?'

She snorted. 'What do you think?'

'If that was hate last night, then hate me some more, Ami Winterburn.'

The blood rose to her face. It was only a kiss, for heaven's sake, she thought in annoyance. But she wasn't in the habit of getting into clinches with unsuitable men, however attractive, and it was the second time it had happened. She averted her eyes from North Kendrick's self-satisfied smile, finding it very easy to hate him.

'Your friend Emma is either very confident or very beautiful,' he commented, running his hand in a long caress down Spritz's back. Without meaning to, Ami followed the motion, registering a tingle down her own spine.

'She's both. Why?'

His eyes came back to her, roamed from ankles to the top of her head. 'You would make a—distracting feature in anyone's wedding pictures.'

Ami blinked, not entirely pleased. A 'distracting feature' could just as well be a chandelier or a flower arrangement. His compliments always roused this dual pleasure and aversion. It was as if his very admiration was a trap.

His admiration was certainly getting a warm response from Spritz. The dog drooled and grinned at a smiling North, in the unqualified affection that can exist between a human and an animal. The man looked suddenly more relaxed. 'I used to have a dog. A sheepdog. He was very intelligent,' North said, giving Spritz a last pat before he stood up.

'What did you call him?'

'Meg.'

'A boy dog called Meg?'

'Short for Megabyte,' he said, with a faint smile of reminiscence. 'I was precocious and keen on computers.'

'Yes, I heard. The boy genius,' she said, leading the way into the house.

Inside, she dumped her drink bottle down and pulled the elastic from her hair. She shook her head, rubbed at it with a towel. Scowling at North, she said, 'Just for the record, I am not a failed actress.'

'That stung, did it?'

'I've had several good parts.'

'Years ago. In soup commercials. And party turns as a singing telegram girl, whatever that entails. Exotic dancing, perhaps?'

'Even the best performers have back-up careers because it can be hard to stay in work. I got into make-up and special effects as a sideline and it became more fascinating than acting and dancing. It often happens.'

His grey eyes didn't waver. Liar, they seemed to say. 'After all, *you* started off inventing things and now you sit at a desk adding noughts to numbers on paper.'

He frowned at this and she went on curiously, 'What kind of things did you invent?'

North shoved his hands into his pockets. 'Nothing you would recognize. Small electronics components. Inventions are worth nothing unless you get them into production. I spent a couple of years just getting investment funds and finding production partners and the whole thing blew up into a huge operation.'

'And you never did get back to inventing. Do you miss it?'

'Why should I? It was merely a springboard to better things.'

But Ami looked levelly at him and his eyes flicked away to a table that held a head form with a wig foundation partly tufted with black hair. He fingered the hair and grimaced. 'What is this stuff you're sewing on?'

'Not sewing, ventilating,' she said. 'I'm ventilating synthetic hair onto the lace foundation. It's to be an Egyptian pharaoh wig—cheap—for an amateur theatre group I help out now and then. Look, you didn't come to ask questions about wig making.'

Grey eyes held hers. 'No.'

Ami waited a moment and when he remained silent, she spread her hands in a silent invitation to go on. North followed her hand movements as he always seemed to and something in his eyes made her heartbeat quicken. Now that the glow of exercise was diminishing, she felt a chill tingle along her spine and down between her breasts. 'Well?' she prompted, huskily.

'Do you know where Harry is?'

Ami blinked in surprise. 'No. Don't you?'

His mouth compressed. 'Has he phoned you?'

'No,' she said. Then, flippantly, 'Don't tell me Harry has run away from home?'

His head went back and he looked down his nose. 'Harry told me he was going home by cab last night, but my information is that it was you who dropped him off at the hotel. So you were the last person to speak to him. I ask again, have you seen him or heard from him?'

My information. Hands on hips, she said, 'And I'm telling you again, no, I have not. I left him at the car park elevator.'

'But then, you are a first-class liar. You won't mind if I look around?'

He headed off down the hall, pushing wide the doors the way he had that other time. Ami followed indignantly. 'Yes, I do mind. Harry's not hiding in my wardrobe!'

He looked suspiciously around her bedroom before his gaze came to rest on her unmade double bed. Any other day of the week it would be chastely made up and smoothed by now, but it was Saturday, the day she changed the sheets, and the pillows were awry and the bedclothes in the rumpled state occasioned by her sprawling sleeping habits. Her bed always looked as if two people, not one, had slept in it, a fact not lost on North Kendrick.

'Heavy night?' he drawled.

Ami flushed. She looked him in the eye and reached past him to close her door with an eloquent little snap. 'Harry's not here.'

'I want you to let me know if he contacts you.'

A vague alarm on Harry's behalf, but she dismissed it. After all, that day on the roof, the old man had shouted that he wouldn't stay where his friends weren't welcome. At present, Harry had no choice but to stay, but he was probably hiding out with a friend somewhere in token independence, to worry North a little, make him feel guilty, even. Harry, she thought without any illusions, was a manipulative old devil. Ami surveyed North's appearance and wondered if it was guilt or concern that had put the bags under his eyes and prevented him from shaving. 'When did you notice he was missing?'

'I got home after two this morning and stopped by his room, found his bed hadn't been slept in. There was no note.'

After two, she thought. The bags and the bristles were more likely the aftermath of some serious socialising in that case. With Francesca, she wondered? In the back seat of that magnolia Jaguar? Ami dismissed the idea. The man owned a hotel full of magnificent rooms. He would not need to resort to the back seat of a car if Francesca tired of an uncomplicated love life while her divorce came through. 'Someone must have seen him leave the hotel. Your paranoid security people? The hawk-eyed Morgan?'

He shook his head. 'He didn't go to his own house, so... I want you to ring me if you hear from him.'

I want again. Deliberately she shrugged one shoulder as she walked into the kitchen. 'I'll think about it.' She snatched up her drink bottle from the counter and tipped it up to drink from it.

'You'd be wise to cooperate unless you want to hear from my lawyers,' he said harshly.

Ami spun around, arms outflung. A few drops of barley water flew from the drink bottle. 'What is it about you Kendrick men? Harry threatens to tell you my real name if I don't perform my pensioner act for his birthday, you threaten to take me to court if I don't cooperate!'

'Ah—he forced your hand, did he? The cunning old devil,' North said, a gleam in his eyes. 'Serves you right.'

'You *admire* that, don't you?' she said incredulously. 'By forcing my hand, he made a complete idiot of you, but even so you can't help admiring him for getting the better of me. *Men*!'

'You might lose the game, but you have to appreciate the skill of the other players,' he said with what he clearly believed was inarguable logic.

Ami shook her head, baffled by the ability of males to fight with each other yet at the same time remain their own greatest fans.

'Well, I don't find blackmail and manipulation admirable. Don't either of you ever just *ask* people to do things for you—say "would you please" instead of "I want"? But then, maybe you both like the buzz of making people jump through hoops!'

'It worked. You did stay for his birthday,' he pointed out mockingly as if the blackmail was justified by the result. 'It can only have been sympathy for him or fear of me that did the trick. And even Harry couldn't have commanded your sympathy in such a short time.'

Ami laughed. '*Fear*? Don't imagine there is anything about you personally that I fear, North. Only your influence. You have power and like most men you abuse it. I fear *that*.' North didn't like that, she noticed.

He sneered. 'On the other hand, maybe you did it because you enjoyed it. As part of your varied career, have you often dressed up to entertain men for their birthdays? Or even,' he added, flicking an insolent glance over her body, 'dressed down?'

Ami drew in an audible breath and let it out in a hiss. She jerked her hand towards him and liquid from her drink bottle shot out in an arc over his face and chest.

CHAPTER SIX

BARLEY water dripped from his hair. It ran in rivulets over the concave planes of his cheeks, along his bristly jaw to drip from his chin. Impassively, he looked down at his drenched sweater, tweaked the fabric between finger and thumb.

'Oh,' she said lamely. 'Here—have my towel.' She dragged it from around her neck and thrust it at him and he flinched, as if this might be some new attack. Regarding her through spiky lashes, he took the towel, mopped his face.

'That was inexcusable,' he said at last.

'Don't you lecture *me* on behaviour,' she said heatedly out of combined pique and guilt.

'I mean, what I said was inexcusable.'

Ami opened and shut her mouth. With a lopsided smile, he added, 'I wonder why we seem to bring out the worst in each other.'

And while she was still adjusting to this philosophical reaction to having a drink flung in his face, he looped the towel over her shoulder, crossed his arms and pulled off his sweater so that she was suddenly confronted with a half-naked North Kendrick. She had an impression of a wide, deep chest with a spattering of dark hair on tan skin as he turned away. Perfunctorily, he said, 'Do you mind?' and proceeded to wring his wet sweater over the basin. In the course of her mixed career Ami had seen a great many men without their shirts, some of them famous for their physique. So why she should find the sight of this man, performing a homely task at her kitchen sink, so riveting, she couldn't say. It was true, he was very nicely built. Without clothes, he looked much bigger, more muscular. She watched the flex and play of muscle in his upper back as he shook out the sweater. His shoulders rose and fell with the action, and, with his arms held up as he inspected the sweater for damage, made one of those irresistible contour lines so persuasively male. Power and beauty together, she thought, frankly admiring the bulge of biceps and his smooth, lightly tanned skin.

He flipped the wet sweater over one shoulder and took up a leaning stance against the counter. Pure James Dean, she thought derisively. The charismatic drifter look. If he had seemed formidable in his high-priced suit in his high-priced hotel foyer, now he looked positively dangerous with his unshaven jaw and his damp hair hanging over his forehead. From one kind of power to another, she thought. It was so unfair.

'I apologize,' he said.

For a confused moment she thought he was apologizing for his sex appeal. In the few blank moments when she stared at him, he gave a cat-got-the-cream smile, nodded at the drink bottle on the counter. 'I hope there's no drink left in that thing. I'm getting nervous with you staring at me like that.'

Which was as good a way as any to let her know that he knew she was gaping at him. 'You're safe,' she said ambivalently. 'Unless you insult me again.'

'I suppose I should apologize for that other comment, too—prompted by the state of your bed.'

'I suppose you should,' she said tightly. 'It's none of your business whether I've had a heavy night or not.'

'Put it down to jealousy,' he said. 'I wish it was me who had rumpled your sheets.'

She might have thought she hadn't heard right, except that his expression confirmed his words. Ami felt the attraction, the magnetism of the man, the flutter of her own pleasure at his earthy statement of desire. He was handsome, wealthy, powerful and many women probably lost their head when such a man announced his intentions. Ami made a concerted effort to keep hers as he turned to leave, and she followed him to the door, unable to avoid the sight of his lovely bare back and his rear, jauntily encased in denim. A weakness made her knees waver. I want him, she thought in astonishment, and she imagined herself laying her hands on that broad back, sliding them into the back pockets of his jeans... So compelling was it, that she rushed, breathless, to get him out, reaching past him for the door. He looked at her arm.

'You give lessons in illusion on a Saturday?' he mocked, indicating the four-day-old bruise inside her elbow. 'Or can't you bear to wash off your own work?'

'Your work, actually,' she said, before she thought.

'What?' Startled, he took her arm and looked closer at the real bruise inside her elbow. 'I didn't see this last night.'

'I'm a make-up *girl*,' she mocked, intensely conscious of his touch. 'I can make a bruise go where there isn't one, and I can conceal a real one. You didn't see it because I didn't want it seen.'

As he assimilated how and when he might have done it, he took her other arm and found the matching mark there. A dull flush settled on his cheekbones and he stood there holding her arms, his thumbs circling gently on the discolourations as if he might erase them. The sensation reached beyond the skin he touched, rippled down her spine, zipped along her temples to the top of her head. Ami touched her tongue to her lower lip and, as if he was waiting for some such signal, North raised her left arm and bent to put his mouth to the bruise. He didn't take his eyes off her, and she stared at him, bemused, her eyelids flickering in response to the warm, delicate touch of his lips on her skin. Ami jumped at the sly touch of his tongue. Low down in her body she felt again that pang of desire. Still holding her gaze, confident now and deliberate, he reached for her other arm and Ami backed away in alarm, wondering if she'd been hypnotized. She felt vaguely disappointed that the glimpse of sincerity in him had been so soon eclipsed by opportunism.

North smiled. 'If it's any consolation, you gave me a bruise, too, that night, when you felled me.'

Oh, good, she thought. 'Well, I won't offer to kiss it better.'

He laughed softly, showing his very nice teeth. 'I should be so lucky.' He rubbed one lean flank, to indicate the position of the bruise, and Ami felt another jolt of sensation at the earthiness of it. She had vastly underestimated North Kendrick, she realized, as she opened her front door and let him out to a joyous welcome from Spritz. His lack of people skills did not prevent him being expert at seduction. But then seduction didn't actually come under people skills. More an exercise in appreciation, like the expertise of the wine connoisseur or the art collector. North Kendrick wanted her for the same reason that she had needed to get through his glass doors. They both wanted to restore their self-esteem by making their mark on the other's territory. But for her, the territory had been his hotel. For him, *she* was the territory.

Marvellous, she thought, as she got on with her chores when he was gone. He had accused her of insinuating herself into his life, but the man had insinuated himself into hers. The kitchen wasn't quite the same now that he'd stripped half naked in it, and as for the bedroom... Ami ripped the old sheets from the bed for washing, and replaced them with fresh ones. *I wish it was me who'd rumpled your sheets.* 'Huh!' she said out loud, energetically smoothing rumples from the clean sheets to erase any images of him in her bed. Then she had another, irrelevant vision of North, coming in at two in the morning and stopping by Harry's room. Did he always stop by his father's room when he came home? Did he tiptoe? Sneak the door ajar so as not to disturb the old man? North as the concerned, caring son? She slid the pillows into new cases and bashed them into a huddled group. She smoothed the quilt cover, catching sight of the bruises on her arms with every move. Later, when she'd hung out her washing and showered, she used some flesh-coloured concealer over the bruises. When she'd finished, she viewed the results with professional satisfaction. No one would know there were bruises there. No one except her and North Kendrick.

North swivelled his chair to look down at the hotel concourse. He waited for the thrill of possession, of fulfilled ambition but it was wearing off already. He grimaced. Even a year ago, he'd still experienced an intense pleasure from bringing off new deals, making new acquisitions, fulfilling ambitions that had once seemed laughable. This hotel was one of them. A foolish venture in some ways, when he could have simply bought a profitable existing hotel and management package, or pumped funds into an unprofitable one. Plenty of those around at present. But it was a long time since his inventive days and he'd wanted to build something he could actually see, so he had, against all advice. Not with his own hands, of course, but with his brain and acumen and powers of persuasion with his investors. He'd expected it to be the greatest thrill of his life, but somehow it was falling rather flat. Maybe he should take up parachuting—an adrenalin-high sport—as an antidote to boredom.

The phone buzzed and he flicked a switch. 'Mr. Kendrick,' a harried female voice said. 'I'm from room service. I just took some of your father's favourite cake up for morning tea and—I'm sorry, but he's gone.'

North felt the sting of anxiety. 'Gone? Again?' He sighed. 'All right. Thank you. Leave it with me.'

He went through the routine again. Checked for a note, checked with floor staff, with Morgan. Someone in the kitchens remembered an 'old geezer' passing through with walking sticks. No-one knew where Harry had gone this time. No-one, North thought grimly, knew where he'd been last time. He'd arrived back two days later and said he'd been looking up a few friends he hadn't seen since the old days, and chances were that's where he'd gone again. North didn't know who they were. A fear that hadn't finished growing gnawed at his insides, but he refused to give it a name. Instead, he applied himself to the problem. Harry must have told someone where he'd been. He was a talker and it wasn't natural for Harry to be so close-lipped. So who would he confide in? He thought of confidences and inevitably thought of Ami who had heard so many of his own. He knew Harry had phoned her. Yes. Ami Winterburn would know something. Logically, he should wait a little longer in case Harry turned up, but he convinced himself he should speak to Ami as soon as possible. It was nearly two weeks since he'd seen her, leaping along the footpath with her dog.

North felt a rush of exhilaration, as if he'd been pumped full of a stimulant or parachuted out the hatch. He felt the challenge as if she'd looked right through him with those fey aquamarine eyes, taunted him with one of those extravagant hand movements. Right now, she was probably out in her back room at her shop, creating a scar on the back of her hand or showing someone how to look bald.

But Ami wasn't at the shop. Ami was conducting her Thursday class, Helen said dubiously, but when he worked on her a little, she gave him the address. With a new surge of energy, he ordered his car to be brought to the hotel entrance.

The class was being held in an office building at North Sydney. There was a double foyer, the outer one a small jungle of potted plants. Through the glass door, he saw Ami walk into this outer foyer. She rounded the doorway and stepped back against the partition where she was out of sight of her students, whose heads North could just about make out, bobbing beyond a screen. Ami's head went back, her eyes closed and for a few seconds her body sagged before she took a deep breath, gathered herself up. Smiling, she made light-hearted comments as her students passed into the foyer on their way out. Her Thursday class that she had adamantly refused to cancel. He remembered that other Thursday weeks ago, and her reddened eyes that might have been a tribute to her make-up skill, but then again, might not.

The students came through the outer door, and North saw why this was one make-up class she wouldn't cancel even under threat of ruin. That they came out laughing told him more about Ami Winterburn than he'd ever gleaned from his computer enquiries or even from her mother.

The last time he'd seen faces like these had been in a hospital. There were six students, five women, one man, casualties of accident and disease. North had to control the urge to drop his eyes as they glanced at him. He stood there a while, watching them walk away, thinking of different kinds of courage. Thinking of his shallow assumptions about Ami's profession, about Ami herself. His considerable achievements suddenly seemed to shrink compared to this small group of maimed people who could leave Ami Winterburn's class smiling. 'Teaching others to appear what they aren't,' he'd said in lofty ignorance. He cringed at the memory.

He found her as he'd never expected to find the flippant, happy-go-lucky Ami Winterburn. Hunched over her partly packed make-up kit, weeping into a tissue. She turned at the sound of his approach and her eyes widened in surprise. She made no attempt to hide her tears. 'Special effects,' she said with a sniff. 'I'll bet you can't tell them from genuine tears.'

'I saw your students,' he said softly, making short work of that little bit of bravado. She suppressed a hiccup and looked balefully at him. Why had he turned up suddenly out of the blue? North looked at her steadily, the way he had that night when she'd taken off her wrinkles and he'd wanted to know what lay beneath. Well, the man who liked his women beautiful wasn't seeing anyone he would fancy this time, she thought, with fierce satisfaction. Her nose always reddened when she cried, her skin turned blotchy and her eyelids swelled.

Here I am, she thought, facing him squarely, a real, hurting person—not an attractive piece of female merchandise—see how you like this, Mr. North Kendrick. He held her gaze, fished in his pocket and found a folded handkerchief, which he offered to her.

'You can have my shoulder to cry on if you prefer,' he said, when she didn't take the handkerchief.

Ami looked at both his shoulders, outlined in tailored fine wool. She might have admired them but hadn't considered them as anchors in a storm, hadn't thought of North Kendrick as someone she might lean on in a moment of weakness. Her heart beat faster. She plucked the handkerchief from him and he gave a sardonic smile at her choice.

Ami dabbed her eyes and blew her nose noisily. 'I run several cosmetic therapy courses each year. Every time I start a six-week course, I think, this time I can handle it, and most times I can. I've made it through to the fifth week this time without—' She waggled her fingers at her teary face. 'They don't want sympathy, just practical solutions.' She turned away to slot tubes and jars into their allotted places in her fold-out make-up case.

She swallowed hard, busied herself with fastening the case. But this time the tears wouldn't stop coming.

'You can't drive in that state,' North said and took her arm. 'There's a deli across the road. I'm buying you a coffee.'

The delicatessen had an alcove with low lights and canvas chairs. The air was steamily warm, scented by ground coffee beans, fresh bread and the bunches of drying rosemary and thyme that hung over their marble-topped table. North ordered coffee and sandwiches. He took off his jacket, loosened his tie and sat back, saying nothing as Ami blew her nose again.

'Tell me,' he said.

Ami blinked at the bald invitation. 'One of my students. Miranda. Eighteen. She was in a car accident and her face was badly scarred. Her boyfriend saw her in hospital when the bandages came off and never came back. Her father cries when he sees her. She's a bright kid with heaps of personality and humour and courage but people are treating her as if she's lost the only thing that matters...her *looks*. Suddenly she's the invisible woman. She keeps talking about how plastic surgery might make her pretty again.'

'And will it?'

'Probably. You can get rid of the *external* scars sometimes. But once you've been invisible you must always be afraid you'll fade away again.'

He looked thoughtfully at her, reached across and laid his hand over hers in a warm, human touch that could not translate into actual words. Ami stared at him. She didn't want sympathy, either. Ami wasn't sure just what she did want, but incredible as it seemed, at this moment, North Kendrick came close to filling the bill. *Tell me.* No spurious sentiment from North, no clichéd comfort, or slick phrase to sum up the tragedy of an eighteen-year-old girl. At least he recognised the depth of his ignorance on the subject and gave it the respect of keeping quiet, unlike many people. Or maybe it was a lack of feeling that kept him quiet. The only time he'd shown strong feelings was when his own life was touched. Maybe he didn't feel for others. But Ami looked down at his hand over hers and experienced a sense of comradeship that she surely could never have with someone so disabled. Intuitively she felt they were on the same wavelength. Startled, she met his eyes. He was serious, silently enquiring. As the moment went on, though, his eyes subtly warmed, his nostrils flared and his head raised a fraction, like a hunter sniffing the wind. Flushed, she pulled her hand from beneath his. This was the man who loved a challenge, she reminded herself. There was more than one way to a conquest for a clever man like North.

She put away the damp handkerchief. 'How's Harry?' she asked.

North took some time putting down his coffee cup.

'I thought you might tell me,' he said levelly. 'He's gone again.'

She didn't quite hide a laugh. At seventy-one, Harry had become the worrisome runaway teenager and North his anxious keeper.

He glowered at her. 'You think this is funny?'

'I think you take your responsibilities seriously. Maybe Harry is trying to tell you that he's not ready to be your responsibility.'

'He's not my *responsibility*—he's my father.'

Ami looked more carefully at him. 'When he's ready, I'm sure he'll turn up again, like he did last time,' she said.

North toyed with a teaspoon, digging it into the sugar to load it, holding it up a little to let the sugar trickle out. He had a worried look of concentration that reminded her of the photo of him as a child, in the sand with his bucket and spade.

'He's been trying to trace old pals of his, writing to relatives he hasn't been in touch with for decades.' He shovelled sugar with dedication. 'Amost as if he's—tying up loose ends.'

A man of seventy-one, tying up loose ends? Ami felt a pang of anxiety, closely followed by denial. Not Harry—she couldn't lose Harry, not when she'd only just met him. 'He's just been in hospital, probably had time to think about all the things he's been too busy to do and decided to catch up on old friends and family. A crisis can make you value those things.'

'Yes, you're probably right,' he said, visibly relaxing.

'He said you were trying to talk him into selling his house,' she said, striving to keep any hint of criticism from her voice.

He gave a rueful laugh. 'Talking Harry into anything is more difficult than I imagined. I haven't seen a lot of him over the past ten years. I'd forgotten how determined he can be. He sets his mind on something and doesn't let go until he has his way.'

'Like father, like son?' she said dryly.

His eyes glittered. 'I usually get what I want.'

'Even if you have to deprive someone else,' she mocked, thinking of the business opponents who had cause to regret his determination.

His smile uncurled, slow and languid as smoke. 'I don't think someone else would necessarily feel *deprived*,' he said, obviously not thinking of his business opponents.

Ami lifted her cup a little too quickly and froth slipped down the side. 'How would you ever know? Do you ask the people you've taken over if they feel deprived? Do you ask your *conquests* if they mind being conquered?'

His irritating complacency grew. 'I've had no complaints.'

'Maybe they fake it.'

And the reminder of her own successful faking took the complacent tilt off his handsome mouth. Ami regarded him over her coffee cup, pleased that she still had an edge. She felt a sudden, urgent need for it because she was treading dangerous paths, imagining him as a lover and herself as his. Stupid, when she knew his pursuit was more to do with payback than love or desire. Maybe nothing short of possessing her would restore him, that age-old symbol of triumph and male superiority. She set her cup down hard. Coffee slopped onto the table.

'It must be difficult for Harry, being immobilized,' she said to correct this dangerous detour. 'I get the impression he's always been very active.'

North acknowledged the retreat with a quizzical smile.

'Active is an understatement. He used to take the back steps three at a time, he had so much energy. I remember him climbing up to lop the poinciana tree, hefting an axe—he used that axe to cut down a Christmas tree every year, too—' North picked up a teaspoon, turned it over and over, looking into the distorted reflections as if it was showing him pictures of the past.

'You had them growing—Christmas trees?'

'We used to drive out towards the Blue Mountains to a farm every Christmas Eve. The best part of Christmas—walking around the paddock of pines, deciding which tree.'

'And Harry cut it down?'

'A couple of strikes with the axe and—' North used the side of his hand to recreate Harry's decisive strikes and the toppling of the tree, with the male appreciation for technique. 'Harry was very good at things like that. A natural athlete. He rode in bike hill scrambles and that's as rough as it comes.'

'You *do* remember his racing days, then?'

He gave a snort. 'Does a kid forget a thing like that? I used to go and watch him race, work on the bikes with him, when he'd let me, until we just seemed to... for competitions he wore long, black bike boots with straps and silver buckles.' A faraway smile transfigured his face. 'God, how I wanted those boots—you know the way a kid covets adult things. They were huge, but Harry used to tell me one day I might be big enough to fit into them.' He gave an odd self-deprecatory smile. 'When I saw him in hospital, then in the wheelchair, I couldn't believe it. He'd changed—I don't know, grown smaller or something, and I hadn't noticed. The only thing that hasn't changed is that he's just as hard to get along with,' he said, his mouth set. Ami studied him, thinking of his irritation so hard on the heels of barely disguised hero-worship.

'Are you annoyed with Harry for getting old?' she asked.

North looked at her in dislike. 'No, I am not *annoyed* with Harry for getting old,' he mimicked. He tossed the teaspoon onto the table and studied her for a few unnerving seconds. 'Your mother told me your father is a doctor.'

'A surgeon. Didn't your credit card investigation tell you that?' she mocked.

'She also told me about her agency and her writer client. Your mother said you often take on unusual jobs.'

'My mother seems to have said a great deal.'

The merest flicker of his eyelids gave him away. Ami grinned. 'She's hard to stop once she gets started, isn't she? Serves you right. Did she persuade you to part with a nymph for the raffle?'

'I've agreed to a painting. We're... negotiating on the nymph,' he said straight-faced. 'Shall we go?'

Negotiating. Ami didn't like the ongoing sound of it.

Outside on the pavement, he turned to her and said, 'If Harry contacts you I would appreciate a call. I'd— just like to know that he's okay.'

I would appreciate. Not *I want*. North must be more worried than she thought. 'Is there something you're not telling me about Harry's departure this time?'

He studied the passing traffic for a moment. 'He didn't take any clothes and he left his wheelchair behind,' he said, his brow creasing. North shuffled his feet and bent an intense gaze on a boutique window display. 'I wouldn't be so concerned about that except that he had his solicitor call around the other day. To finalise a few things, he said.' North hesitated then went on. 'It sounds stupid, I know, but sometimes I'm afraid he might—' North took a deep breath and sidestepped the obvious phrase as if to name it would be to make it more possible. 'He seems rather...depressed,' he said lamely. 'I thought he might be hiding some condition from me, something incurable, but I talked to his doctor and she said there is nothing like that.'

'Harry wouldn't do anything silly,' she said but she remembered something Harry had said. *There'll be no more birthdays after this one*. And, *It's too late for that, now*. Something must have shown in her face for North took her arm and said, 'What's the matter?'

'It's nothing. Where did you see him last? What was he doing?'

'On the terrace, looking through those binoculars.'

Something stirred in Ami's memory. Harry and the binoculars and something he'd said. 'He showed me a hotel he'd worked on as a young man,' she offered slowly. 'Said it still operated as a hotel and he would like to see it again. I wonder...'

They drove to the Avalon in North's magnolia Jaguar. Ami stood on North's terrace and searched with binoculars for the old hotel building Harry had shown her. It took her nearly ten minutes to locate it. 'There,' she said. 'I can just make out the name—the Century.'

*   *   *

Harry was seated at the bar of the Century Hotel, walking sticks leaning against his stool. He had a schooner of beer in one hand, a forbidden cigarette in the other, and looked far from suicidal. He broke off from a conversation with the barman when he saw North and Ami and made an involuntary effort to hide the cigarette before he defiantly changed his mind and flaunted it. 'What are you two doing here?'

'Harry—are you okay? Why didn't you tell me where you were going? You left your wheelchair, you'll end up in hospital again,' North said in a tight, scolding tone that failed to convey the concern Ami had so clearly seen.

Irritation flitted over the old man's face. 'I don't have to tell you what I'm doing every minute,' he said mulishly. 'I just came down here for a drink and to look at the work I did on that cedar panelling, see? I'll be back for dinner, all right? You're a sight for sore eyes, Amelia,' he added, his faded blue eyes sharply speculative about her arrival with North. The following communication between the two men was terse. All North's stiff persuasion failed to move the old man, who said he would call a cab and come home when he was good and ready.

North was silent as he drove her back to pick up her car. Ami glanced several times at his profile, which relief had rendered no less severe. 'Those boots Harry used to wear for bike racing,' she said lightly, for something to say. 'Did they live up to your expectations when you eventually grew into them?'

North concentrated on swinging the Jaguar in next to her car. 'I never got to try them. Harry gave them away when I was sixteen,' he said, glancing at her.

'Oh.'

North opened the door for her, walked to her car with her.

'Thank you for your help,' he said. 'I wouldn't have believed Ami Winterburn could contribute to my peace of mind, but today, you have.'

'Ah, well, you don't know me very well,' she said lightly.

'No. That might take more time than I thought.' He eyed her with a certain calculation that made her think of takeovers and financial coups.

'More time than you're prepared to spend,' she told him. 'I am very complex.'

'I'm a quick study. I was a boy genius, remember?'

Smug devil. She resented the way he made her feel frail and hunted. Let him hunt. She wasn't going to fall for his strategies. Getting to know her wasn't his aim, except in the biblical sense. 'You can forget it, North,' she snapped. 'You aren't going to rumple my sheets!'

He burst out laughing and for the first time it was audible, a pleasant, tenor sound that was warm and uncomplicated. How very amusing he found her, she thought wrathfully.

'I mean it, North,' she said. 'It was the purest accident that we met. You are definitely not my type.'

His expansive good humour disappeared in a hurry, she was delighted to see. Mr. North Kendrick, handsome, rich, eligible, was used to judging women but not, perhaps, used to being judged unsuitable himself. 'I wonder how you kiss men who *are* your type,' he said sardonically. 'The poor devils must melt down in the heat.' When she didn't respond, he said, 'Well—if I'm not your type, I have to accept it. I don't make a habit of pursuing women who don't want to be pursued.'

Ami regarded him with suspicion. 'Very civilized of you.'

'But why don't we agree to a truce relationship, for Harry's sake?' He held a hand out to her and she looked at it, her back against her car and an odd feeling that she might as well have been against a brick wall. 'He's

fond of you. It would be silly if you felt you couldn't
visit him because of any, er, tension between us.'

'I'm surprised you'd encourage my friendship with
Harry, considering the way I met him. Doesn't it have
unpleasant associations for you?'

'And some extremely pleasant,' he said with a nostalgic air.

'This doesn't sound like a truce relationship to me.'

'Will it help if I don't mention the pleasure you've
brought me?' he enquired. 'What else should I not
mention? Your eyes—your mouth...' He leaned an arm
on her car so that his face was tilted quite close to hers.
'Better not mention your hair, your legs, those arm
movements...'

'If you think I'm flattered by this, I'm not,' she said,
fighting the candlelight mood he was generating in a
parking lot in brilliant sunshine. 'I'm a great deal more
than superficial things like legs and—and green eyes. I'm
a lot of other things, too, an entire person, not just a
collection of curvy bits like your sculptures. So don't
imagine you're going to add me to your collection.'

'That's not what I imagine,' he told her, his grey eyes
warm. It would be so easy to have a physical affair with
North Kendrick. She would hate herself for it afterwards. But oh, she would love it for a little while.

Colouring, she said tartly, 'What did you mean—arm
movements?'

He straightened, threw his arms wide in mimicry of
her habitual gesture. His teeth showed in a smile that
took her breath away. 'I get this mad urge to run into
them.'

He had always stared at her when she did that, she
remembered, right from the start. North Kendrick,
running into her arms. It should be ludicrous but it
wasn't, it was appealing. Her heart beat heavily, faster.
A mad urge. She hadn't thought of him as a man who
had mad urges... She caught herself in time.

He was very, very good. Her face flamed as she turned away to set the key in the lock. North had simply changed tactics. She was being shown an example of the long-term planning for which he was famous. If he had any mad urge associated with her, it was a very basic one.

So when he held out his hand again, she took it for Harry's sake, understanding that North's idea of a truce was simply another move in the game. And as long as she knew that, she was in no danger, was she? His hand closed strongly around hers and he looked into her eyes with some indefinable expression that made her assurance seem foolhardy.

'Come to dinner tomorrow. With Harry, of course,' he said.

'Sorry, I can't. I have an appointment with the dressmaker. My bridesmaid's dress. It's urgent because the wedding's only a couple of weeks away, and it's out west so I have to be ready to leave days before,' she said, babbling out unnecessary excuses. 'Some other time?'

She drove away thinking that almost every female she knew would think she was crazy to turn down Kendrick. One part of her said, well—why not let it take its course? However base North's motivation, he would be a great lover. He treated his collector's items very well, while he treasured them. She screeched to a halt at traffic lights, wishing she could relegate him to the ranks of the purely superficial. But she thought instead of North, the cool, level-headed man of business, worried about losing his father. And she thought of the father who'd been such a forgetful hero that he'd given away to someone else something he'd promised his son.

She was moved, as she always was by North's vulnerable side. 'Oh, grow *up*!' she said out loud. The man had had too much power too soon and was unbearable. He was a collector, remember that. And anyway, he was probably a lousy lover.

CHAPTER SEVEN

AMI slid under her car. It had been quite cool that morning when she and Harry had set out after their overnight stop, quite tolerably warm by the time she had dropped him off at Swagman's Creek, to which tiny country town he had traced yet another of his old cronies. But when she'd travelled on alone, the day had heated up as midday approached and passed. Ami had developed a parched, painful throat and a nagging headache from the dust and hot air. At least, she thought, it was marginally cooler *under* the car.

She unrolled the canvas tool kit, more to counter the dismal feeling of helplessness than anything. Somehow she felt the exact nature of the damage was more likely to reveal itself to someone with a spanner or a hammer in their hand.

'Ugh,' she muttered, wiggling around a spill of some oily black substance. She had only pulled over for a few minutes to drink some water and take an aspirin, and when she had headed back to the road the wheels had dipped into a rut and the car had hit something. In vain, she tried to see signs of damage but realized she would need the torch.

As she slid out again, she heard the scrape of leather on stones. In the aperture between the ground and the underside of the car, she saw clumps of grass crushed beneath two shoes. Help, at last. Hastily, she wriggled out, almost blinded in the sunlight after minutes in comparative darkness. The shoes were attached to widely planted legs clad in denim. A buckle glinted between two large hands clasped around the leather of a belt.

Glare hazed the man's face but she recognized those hands. She lay flat on the stony ground, heart hammering, wondering if this was one of those famous outback mirages. Because North couldn't be here. He was on a business trip in Malaysia, according to Harry. Expected to be away five days.

'Very appetizing,' he said, looking over her bare legs, the crumpled shorts, the thin cotton shirt, soaked with perspiration and clinging to her breasts. 'But asking for trouble on a lonely road.'

She scrabbled to leap up and her head didn't quite clear the car underside. A hollow clang echoed inside her head as she hit herself, but she yanked the black denim cap down on her head and shook off North's helping hand to stagger up fighting, a spanner in her hand.

'Asking for trouble? *Appetizing*?' she rasped. 'I've been stranded here for over an hour, waiting for help! My hands are a mess—' She thrust out her greasy hands that were cut and grazed. 'Half a million flies have discovered I'm the only moving thing for miles around and I haven't got anything left to drink!' She threw the spanner down in a fine temper and put her hands on her hips. 'And all you can do is leer and tell me I'm asking for trouble by being provocative enough to wear *shorts* in one-hundred degree heat! *Trouble*?' she yelled in his face. 'I've already got trouble, so you can take your leer and your damned male superiority and shove off!'

Her voice screamed on the still, hot air. Ami heard the note of hysteria in it and hoped she wasn't going to cry. North slowly removed his sunglasses and blinked at her, a slight frown cutting above his handsome nose. And even as she noticed the beguiling look of concern in his grey eyes, half his face disappeared. In panic, she reached out to him, grasping his solid shoulder. 'I can't see you properly. North, what's happening? I can't *see* you!'

He made some exclamation, took her by the arm. 'Sit down.'

'North?' she said, on a rising note. She screwed up her eyes, rubbed at them and one of her hands came away sticky and warm with blood. Her knees went weak and she sat down under the pressure of North's hands on her shoulders. She heard him walk away, open a car door, and she called in sudden panic, swivelling her head for a partial view of him. 'Where are you going? Don't leave me. Oh, you rotten, chauvinistic swine. I suppose you'll take me at my word now and shove off just when I *need* you!' She stood and wiped ineffectually at her clouded eye, thrust her arms out wide in entreaty and yelled, 'North!'

A dark shape loomed up and he said, 'I'm here,' and stepped inside her outstretched arms to pull her close. Her arms went around him and she held on to him and snuffled into his shoulder. After the privations of the day, the frustrations and the pain, it was heaven to let herself go and cry. Home to heaven, she thought irrelevantly, sliding her arms around his back, turning her cheek against his neck so that her lips brushed his warm skin and she smelled the fresh tang of him.

Self-consciously she withdrew her arms from around him and found herself guided onto the ground, nudged against a tree. He removed her cap, used a cloth to wipe her eye and when she blinked again, her sight was blurry but almost back to normal. He showed her a vacuum flask and poured orange juice into the lid. The jangle of ice cubes was a sound so sweet that she felt an overwhelming affection for the man who provided it.

'North Kendrick, I take back all the disagreeable thoughts I've ever had about you,' she said fervently, swamping down half the juice with such enthusiasm that it dribbled down her chin.

'All of them—just for orange juice?' he murmured. 'What would I get for French champagne?'

'There speaks the man of business—looking for a return on everything. Profit from money invested, favours in exchange for gifts. Any advance on French champagne?'

'The world does tend to work that way, doesn't it? But please consider the orange juice a gift. No strings,' he said dryly and, kneeling beside her, opened a first-aid kit. He leaned over to part her hair, walked his fingertips through it until he found the source of the bleeding. He removed a hairpin and took her face in both hands, tipping her head so that he could see. Ami closed her eyes, listened to the buzz of flies and the warble of magpies and the deep silence of the countryside. She felt the heat of the sun, dappled on her skin, and the pleasurable, dry warmth of North's large hands across her temples and ears. Nice, she thought hazily, wondering if she might be concussed.

'That blow pressed the hairpin into your scalp and cut the skin. The blood soaked into your cap then trickled down into your eye, blinding you for the moment,' he said, shaking some antiseptic onto cotton wool. The sting of the cut had dulled to a throb and Ami found the tiny tugs on her scalp, the tender progress of his fingers through her hair unexpectedly soothing.

He shifted so that he sat cross-legged beside her, lifting her leg over his knees so that he could clean the grease from a long scratch on her thigh. Ami jumped at the intimate touch. Orange juice slopped over her shorts.

'I can do that myself,' she said.

'Sit still.' He wiped the scratch clean and pressed an adhesive strip over it. Every tiny prod of his fingers produced a flow-on effect, like pebbles tossed into a pool that made ripples and still more ripples. He curved his hands to her thigh and lifted her leg from his knees, then sat, looking her over.

'Better?' he asked.

Better and worse. She nodded. North got up and bent to haul her onto her feet, and the sudden change made her dizzy enough to grab him for support. 'Sorry. I saw stars,' she muttered into the junction of his neck and shoulder, which was hunched into a protective curve for her benefit. She wished she didn't have this absurd wish to touch him there, wished she hadn't clutched at his muscular arms so needily.

North held her with one arm, letting her get her balance, not suspecting, she hoped, that it was achieving the opposite. 'Are you okay?' he said, so close to her ear that she felt the ebb and flow of his breath. He tilted his head downward and his mouth brushed across her temple, her cheek, touched the corner of her mouth. A breeze rippled the tree above and golden flecks of sunlight shimmered on his face as he looked down at her, his eyes gleaming silver, his mouth parted and sensual. She meant to say something prosaic like, 'I'm okay,' or, 'Can you send a breakdown truck,' but she left it too late and North's mouth came down on hers. He kissed her lightly and withdrew, rimmed her lips with the tip of his tongue, leaving them moist and temporarily cooling in the warm breeze, while he pressed his mouth time and again to her neck, her ear. And his hands were in her hair, lightly on her shoulders, sliding beneath the shirt collar. He inched her shirt aside and bent to kiss her exposed shoulder, stroked his mouth along her collarbone and, as she swayed back against the tree, unfastened her shirt buttons and lowered his mouth to the upper curves of her breasts. Ami's head dropped back against the rough bark of the tree. Bright specks of sun dazzled her and giddily she closed her eyes, murmuring her pleasure at North's touch. She stroked the contours of his shoulders and arms, recreating the image of him behind her closed eyelids from touch and smell and the messages jamming the lines of her nervous system. Her fingers trailed along that intriguing line of his shoulder and neck and she smiled dreamily as he shuddered in response. The short hair on the back of his neck bristled beneath her exploring fingers and still she kept her eyes closed, lost in a world of texture and sensation, scarcely able to tell whether it was North, or the breeze, or the sun that touched her skin with exquisite tenderness.

But his hands circled her hips, tipped her towards him in an earthy little movement that penetrated her dreamy self-indulgence. He wanted her, of course he did. Her hands flexed on his fabulous arms, she gave an audible gasp and her eyes flew open to see the gleam of triumph in his. A delicious panic assailed her, a sense of having come to a point of no return. Excitement welled up in her and a desire that rocked her to the soles of her feet.

North unclipped the front of her bra, brushed aside the lace and cradled her breasts in his big hands, bending to draw a nipple into his mouth. Ami's broken sigh of pleasure hung on the hot, still air, was drawn again from her as North repeated the magic. A curious humming sound was in her head, growing ever louder towards crescendo. In mounting passion, she spread her hands on North's backside, traced the hollowed sides and the hard muscularity of his flanks. A growl came from him and Ami exulted in the sound, in the clench of his body against hers. And the humming sound suddenly was a roar with an accompanying rush of airborne dust. A car horn honked and men's voices shouted.

Ami pushed herself away from the tree, clutching at her unfastened bra and shirt. Horn still honking, a truck crawled away down the road with a man leaning from the passenger window and another, in the back of the truck, waving his hat and grinning. North put his hands on his hips and gave a rueful smile. 'No traffic for the past hour and they had to turn up now. Their timing is as immaculate as your mother's.'

Their timing, Ami thought, turning away to fasten her clothes, was about ten minutes too late. Ten minutes?

Was that how long they'd been here, making love under an ironbark tree on the side of the road? Her face turned scarlet. Ten minutes, fifteen. Thirty. She had had no awareness of time passing. She had been in a dream world, all sense and delicacy suspended.

North came close behind her, slid an arm around her waist.

'Okay?' he said softly, dropping a light kiss on her neck. Ami pulled away with such fervour that dizziness overtook her. She put a hand to her head, which was aching badly. Now she was sharply reminded of the sting of cuts and bruises. Her knuckles ached. Her knees and elbows. Everything.

North's eyes narrowed. 'Suddenly you object to me touching you? I thought we'd passed that point.'

She clamped a hand to her head. Concussion. It was the only reason she could have been so daft. '*We* haven't passed any point.'

'We were making love, Ami,' he said. 'In broad daylight, in public and neither of us gave a damn. If the truck hadn't come, we'd still be making love.' His nostrils flared. 'I wish we were. I want you. And you want me.'

She took a step back but he didn't move, just stood there staring at her with that need to possess written on his face, the desire of the collector for another acquisition. And it wasn't just that, she thought, appalled to realize how close she'd come to being collected.

'I'm half concussed,' she snapped. 'And you took full advantage of it, didn't you? Nothing for nothing, that's your motto, North.'

'What the hell are you talking about?'

'You're an opportunist, always looking for a weakness, always working a strategy to get what you want.' She picked up the spanner, the canvas tool kit, and her head swam, but she strode to her car, opening the boot. The tools clanked when she tossed them inside. North came up alongside her.

'Opportunist?' he said between gritted teeth. 'Explain.'

'When I turned up as Amelia, you soon used her to turn a potential disaster into a PR triumph. *Then* you decided to use her as an elderly sounding board for your problems with Harry. Oh, yes. You were quick to find a use for Amelia to compensate for any trouble she cost you. And when I turned up again as myself—you had a use for *me*, too, didn't you? You never waste anything. I should have known when you were playing doctors, tending my wounds, that there would be a price for all that lulling tenderness. You invested precious time anointing my scratches, so why not expect a little return on your investment? After all, that's the way the world works, isn't that what you said?'

North's face was a cold mask, flushed on the cheekbones, white at the corners of his mouth. He reached past her and slammed the boot closed.

'I'm looking for Harry,' he said between his teeth.

'You're always looking for Harry,' she said, hearing the words thicken on her tongue. 'Why did you come all this way?'

'I flew back early. I have a few days unexpectedly spare and I want to spend them with my father,' he snapped. 'At least this time he left me a note to say he was headed in this direction with you. I suppose that's progress. Where is he?'

'He wanted to look up an old mate of his who had moved out west. You were overseas on business, and I was passing through the town on my way to Emma's wedding, so I offered to drop him off. He's with Ken Drummond in Swagman's Creek now. You passed the turn-off a way back.' She waved her hand in the general direction. 'I left him and Spritz there this morning and I'll pick them up on my way back from Catastrophe in three days. That's where my friend is getting married.

I'm supposed to be there tonight,' she said, with a disconsolate look at her stranded car.

He walked to his own vehicle. 'If you want a lift back to Swagman's Creek, get in.'

'I'll wait with my car, thanks,' she said stiffly, then, crushing her pride, said, 'could I ask you to send a tow truck out, please?'

He smiled nastily. 'Aren't you afraid of what it might cost you?'

She watched the frosted magnolia Jaguar go, its image dissolving in the heat waves on the crest of the road. A short time later another image appeared, coming towards her. It was the truck that had passed earlier. The men's grins were detectable from a distance and she was painfully aware of how she must have looked last time they saw her. Half undressed, writhing in a man's arms. And now that man was gone and she was still here. She opened her car door, undecided as to whether this was rescue or trouble, when a horn blasted in the distance and the Jaguar appeared. North had come back.

The truck had slowed, but when the men saw the Jag, they speeded up and passed her, shouting something vulgar about what treats she had missed. If they had been offering rescue, they had been offering trouble first. North's car screeched alongside her, raising a cloud of dust. The passenger door sprang open and Ami got in. She held a hand to her head. It felt fuzzy and ached abominably. The big car turned around and raced towards Swagman's Creek. It was air-conditioned and deliciously cool. No dirt and sweat for North. The seats were softest leather, cushioning her hurts. Home to heaven, she thought yet again. After a while, she glanced at North's granite profile and said, 'Thank you.'

'They were parked on the roadside farther up, eating, and when they saw me pass by alone, they turned back,' he said grimly. 'There are times when I'm ashamed to be male.'

'Maybe they thought I was just a nice girl selling magazine subscriptions,' she said, unable to resist the barb.

North's mouth contracted to the count of ten. 'When we get to the town, you can show me the way to this place where Harry is staying, then I'll drop you at the local garage.'

Ami swallowed hard. Her throat was raw, her head pounded and she thought miserably of having to make arrangements for a tow truck, having to wait around in the heat while repairs were done, when what she really would like was to lie down somewhere cool on a soft mattress. 'Fine. Thanks,' she said hoarsely and felt North glance at her. Her eyes closed and she drifted off into a curious space dotted with bright, sparkly things. After a while, she heard her own voice, counting. ' ...Fifty-one, fifty-two...'

'Fifty-two what?' North said.

'Stars,' she said, opening her eyes. 'I have to count the stars. Oh!' she said in annoyance. 'I shouldn't have opened my eyes. I've lost count—have to start again.' She lay back, closed her eyes. 'One, two...'

The car came to a halt. She felt a hand on her forehead, a delightfully cool hand. Ami took hold of it with both her own and held it to her hot cheek, rubbing against it.

'You're burning up,' North said in a curious voice. 'I'll get some aspirin from the first-aid kit.'

'Burning up,' Ami repeated. 'Never play with fire,' she said solemnly. She swallowed the aspirins he gave her, washed them down with a mouthful of orange juice and closed her eyes. 'Eight, nine, ten—oh!' She gave a groan.

'What is it, Ami?'

'I've lost my place again.'

* * *

The aspirins brought her fever down and she was lucid when North ushered her into a hotel room in the tiny country town where Harry was staying with his friend.

'The doctor will be here soon,' he told her, pushing her down onto the bed. Ami caught sight of herself in the tilted dressing-table mirror. Her hair was matted, flecked with bits of leaf and twig, strands stuck together where North had tried to wash off the blood. Tear stains made a clean track through grease and dirt on her cheeks. Ami bit her lip, made a few half-hearted stabs at tidying her hair and gave up, exhausted. Tears welled in her eyes.

'Lie down,' North said. He pushed her down, lifted her legs onto the bed and leaned over her. 'The fever's rising again.'

There were rust-coloured patches and grease on the shoulder of his lovely, fine cotton shirt, Ami saw. She must have transferred blood and dirt to him when she held her. Staring up at him, she thought vaguely that it was funny for North to kiss such a scarecrow. He liked his women beautiful. 'I look terrible. Nothing like a nice piece of sculpture, not even a chipped one,' she said pugnaciously, in case he thought she didn't know how awful she looked.

'A work of art you are not,' he said dryly.

Ami smiled. 'Good,' she said.

So why on earth did that please her so much? North showed the doctor in and waited outside. Most beautiful women would be riled at such a comment, and even though she was sick, he had meant to rile her. Ami Winterburn. A most contrary woman. And even in a mess, still appealing. In the beginning, he had wanted her for that face, the creamy perfection of her skin, the full, fabulous mouth, the stunning aquamarine eyes. That streaky hair that almost crackled with energy. And he'd wanted her for her dancer's body—tall and slim and athletic. Long legs and those breasts. He closed his eyes briefly and did homage to her breasts. A beautiful woman, Ami Winterburn. A desirable woman. He wanted her. But.

But it wasn't going to be enough, he thought suddenly, in astonishment. To pleasure her and take pleasure from her. It would be extraordinary, exhilarating. His pulses quickened at the mental picture of Ami in his arms, in his bed. Whereas once the picture had been a goal, an end in itself, now he felt a curious incompleteness about it. Not enough? Why not? Now that he knew she wanted him, now that he had come close to having what he wanted from her, there was something else eluding him. Her mind, he thought, trying to get a laugh out of it. How many men thought about Ami Winterburn's mind when that lovely exterior was so distracting? But the truth was, he didn't quite know what or who he was dealing with. Hell, he hadn't even sent her flowers yet. North considered the omission in surprise. It was what he usually did when he was interested in a woman. Flowers. Fly to Melbourne for dinner. Perfume. Eventually jewellery. It all seemed so shallow now, faced with Ami Winterburn. He was a rich man but he had a feeling there was nothing he could buy for her that would impress her. It engendered a reluctant admiration in him, but irritation too because buying things was easy—he had a very efficient gift-buying service for busy executives. All he had to do was phone them, give a description and vital statistics and a perfectly wrapped gift was delivered within hours, with a discreet description of the contents sent to him. He was used to women who responded with approval and pleasure to his merest efforts. Of course the nature of his relationship with Ami was such that it had precluded gifts. She would have tossed them back at him. Perhaps now... He imagined giving her description over the phone to Monica, the gift buyer extraordinaire—how the hell did you describe Ami? Blonde, aquamarine eyes, five foot ten, long neck, long legs, hands that had a language all their own—the obvious features only told half the story, anyway. He imagined those eyes quizzing him steadily over a lavish bouquet of flowers or a flagon of expensive perfume and said out loud, 'Oh, yeah,' unsettling two passing guests. Grinning weakly at them, he thought in dismay that the damned woman had virtually brought on an identity crisis for him. She had made him doubt the worth of his own career, now she was making him feel that even his wealth gave him no advantages. 'Ridiculous,' he said. A passing housemaid threw him a cautious look. North scowled. He was muttering to himself like some old hobo, all because of a make-up girl.

She'd fooled him once and the memory of it still burned. And beneath that wrinkled disguise she'd worn had been the face he'd first seen. The thing was, what was underneath *that* face? Ami refused to fall into any category he'd ever encountered. She was so adept at illusion that she'd made him believe her an old woman, so how would he ever be sure that her current face was the real one? Never one to abandon a line of action once he'd decided upon it, North nevertheless thought it might be wise to back off from Ami Winterburn. There were less complicated ways, more comfortable ways to have a woman in his life, surely. But as he waited, hearing the murmur of her voice through the door, he could only think of Ami, holding out her arms to him in one of those big, embracing gestures she was always making. He'd joked about it with her, using it deliberately to try to seduce her with some small talk. Uncomfortably, he realized that, as usual with a joke, there was truth behind it. He did want to run into her arms. Today, when she'd held them out to him and said she needed him, when she'd rubbed her cheek on his hand like a kitten, he'd felt almost as if... The door opened and the doctor emerged. North was singularly pleased to have his thoughts interrupted.

In her dreams, Ami cried that she would be late for Emma's wedding. North appeared and she grabbed his hand and babbled out her fears that someone would steal her bridesmaid's dress from her abandoned car. Then, in the dream, her dress appeared, covered in plastic. 'Here it is,' North Kendrick said, hanging it on the wardrobe door handle where she could see it. 'Everything is fine.' In her dreams, too, she burned in desert wastelands and stood under cool showers until she shivered. And she argued with North, who wore a cheap checkered shirt and who sometimes stripped her clothes from her, and sometimes dressed her in them again.

But when she eventually woke, the dress for Emma's wedding was hanging on the door handle, just where it had been in the dream, and she wondered if maybe the rest of it had really happened, too. A moment of anxiety passed. But of course, it was all a dream. North Kendrick wouldn't be seen dead in a cheap checkered shirt.

She sat up, feeling seedy but minus the pain that had pounded in her head and body. Anxiously, she went to the bridesmaid's dress, fingering it through the plastic to reassure herself that it was okay. As the door opened, she turned too fast and staggered. 'North,' she said. He caught her around the waist, bent and lifted her. Her hands grabbed at his shoulders, took hold of cotton material coloured blue, red and grey.

'You're wearing a cheap checkered shirt!' she accused.

'Snob,' North said, walking to the bed with her. 'I ran out of clothes and the manager's wife bought it for me at a chain store across the road.' He stood a moment, holding her aloft, looking closely at her. 'No fever. You look better.'

Ami released his shirt, self-consciously felt her hands slide a little over his shoulders. He looked as if he could use a shave. His hair, instead of being neatly brushed back, had fallen in a dark, wavy mass onto his forehead. The checkered shirt fitted closely, she could see the strain on the stiching around his well-muscled shoulders. Ami lifted her fingers from further temptation, tried to find an uncontroversial place to put them, but couldn't. She tried to hunt down the details of those dreams featuring the blue, red and grey shirt but all she could recall was a kaleidoscope of fractured images, most of them involving her naked body. Her colour rose.

'Memory troubling you?' he said, perceptively.

She bit her lip. 'I thought I dreamed the checked shirt, along with all the rest—'

North set her down in a businesslike manner on the tangled sheets of her bed.

'Don't trouble yourself. You were sick. I did what needed to be done, no more, in spite of my opportunistic streak.'

Ami stared at him, surprised to see that it still rankled. He *had* undressed her, looked at her naked, touched her. Ami felt she'd been stripped of more than clothes. She was bereft of defences. This man had started off by watching her while she was in blithe ignorance of him and now he knew things about her that she would never willingly have let him see. Her fists bunched in frustration. North Kendrick already had so much power. Why did fate have to hand him still more?

'Well,' she said stiffly. 'I suppose I should thank you.'

'Don't choke on it,' he said, moving to the door. 'I'll see if the kitchen can rustle you up something to eat. Now that you're better, I'll go visit Harry.'

She nodded, suddenly ravenous. '*Wait*!' she said, as he opened the door. 'What do you mean—you ran out of clothes? How long have I—' she looked over at the other single bed '—we been here?'

'Two nights.'

With a small scream, she slid out of bed. 'Two *nights*! Then today is Friday—Emma's getting married *tomorrow*! And my car—'

'Your car is with the mechanic. It needs parts freighted in from Sydney and will be ready after the weekend.'

'But then—I have to—Emma will be wondering—where are my clothes?' Distractedly, she plucked at her pyjamas, looked around in vain for some street clothes. North put a hand on her shoulder and steered her back to bed.

'I've been giving regular bulletins to Emma. You had her phone number in your diary. She and Matt are expecting you there tonight, so be a good girl and go back to bed.'

She glared at him. 'Don't patronise me. I have to make arrangements to get there. Hire a car—'

'No hire cars available, I asked,' he said smoothly. 'I'm driving you.'

'But it's a hundred miles away,' she objected, thinking of a hundred miles in the magnolia Jaguar with North, a prospect both intriguing and offputting. 'And how will I get back here?'

'The same way. I've talked so often to Emma and Matt, we're practically old friends. They've invited me to their wedding. Isn't that nice?'

'Emma—how could you invite him to the wedding?' Ami said in an undertone to her friend that night.

'How could I not?' said Emma. 'He was nursing you on your sickbed, offering to bring you here because your car was defunct. Besides, he sounded nice.' Emma's eyes strayed to North, who appeared to have struck up an instant rapport with the groom. And why not, Ami thought darkly. Matt Mackenzie was another arrogant male used to getting his own way, even if falling for Emma had brought out his better side. She deliberately recalled Mackenzie as he'd been two years back, raging into her shop looking for Ami, rather than the sensitive man who'd had to come to terms with the loss of a close friend just months ago.

'Nice?' Ami hissed. 'People who are used to having anything they want when they want it are rarely nice. He's a very successful manipulator and his strategies don't end at his office desk. North Kendrick never stops doing deals.'

'What deal was he doing when he was sponging your fevered brow?'

Ami flushed. 'I know I sound ungrateful, but you don't know him. There are no free lunches as far as North is concerned. Both he and his father do it—manipulate people.'

'That's not what's troubling you,' Emma said, eyeing Ami shrewdly. 'You've already half fallen for him, haven't you?'

'Half fallen is a retrievable position,' Ami said stoutly, not bothering with denials to this friend who knew her very well. 'I could never really fall for a man unless I knew he could see more about me than my face and figure.'

Her friend pulled a face. 'You mean you could believe in his sincerity if you were plain and dumpy?'

'That's just the point. I wouldn't have any problem with North if I was plain and dumpy. I'd be invisible to him.'

'You have the same problem as the original poor little rich girl. The only way she can ever be sure a man wants her for herself and not her money, is to get rid of the money,' Emma said, her gaze settling fondly on her husband-to-be. 'Men are such complicated creatures— they often hide the best about themselves and flaunt the worst. If you think he's so superficial and you've half fallen for him anyway, maybe your intuition is trying to tell you something.'

'My intuition, ha! If women's intuition is so good, why aren't we running the world?'

The four of them had drinks on the veranda and watched the stars come out.

'Do you think it will rain tomorrow?' Emma said wistfully, as many a bride must have said on the eve of her wedding.

Matt Mackenzie studied the sky with an experienced eye.

'Not a chance,' he said.

'Oh, darn,' Emma said with a sigh. Ami laughed softly. At North's look of surprise, Emma said by way of explanation, 'Mackenzie grew up in a drought. We're both rather partial to rain.' She and Mackenzie exchanged a slow, smouldering smile. 'But we'll just have to make do with sunshine.'

Emma Spencer and Matt Mackenzie were married in the sunshine, in the courtyard of his homestead, Falkner's Place. Matt looked magnificent in formal clothes, Emma glowed in ivory silk, flowers in her plaited hair. A lump in her throat, Ami stood alongside Steve Mackenzie, the best man. Emma had planned never to marry again after a disastrous attempt years earlier, but blunt, bearlike Matt Mackenzie had changed her mind. If ever there was a moment that confirmed the existence of real love, this was it. It had grown from many things—instant attraction, friendship, hardship and passion, and in the end, patient compromise on the part of both of them to overcome a host of difficulties and delays. They had literally run through fire together. Matt and Emma looked in each other's eyes and made their promises from the heart. They were lovers and friends. There was mutual respect and liking as well as love between them. Their marriage would be built on bedrock, Ami thought, feeling a twinge of envy. That's what I want. She glanced around until she saw North's black hair and hawkish profile. That, or nothing.

It was some time after the formalities before she came across North in the crowd. 'Your scars have vanished,' he said. 'Is that a quick healing process, or a demonstration of your gift for illusion?'

He had borrowed a tuxedo from one of Matt's many friends and it was a little old-fashioned and, she noticed crossly, very fitting around the shoulders. Ami drank a large mouthful of punch, her intuition twanging like a bow that had just released an arrow. Half fallen was a retrievable position, she'd told Emma. Oh, lord, what a fool she was. If she was anywhere else, she would cut and run right now. But it was her best friend's wedding and she couldn't walk out. If North asked her to dance, she would be ready with a refusal.

'Oh, it's pure illusion,' she said, rallying with a light tone and holding out her hand to display the touched-up scars. 'The scars are still there. You can see them if you look closely.'

'You carry that theatrical bag of tricks the way a doctor carries his medical bag,' he said, and, looking at a very brown, very lined woman in her sixties, said dryly, 'I'm tempted to think that's more of your work and that she's really only twenty-six.'

Emma laughed. 'No. Joyce is Matt's aunt, the genuine article.'

'The genuine article,' he repeated, giving Ami an odd look that skimmed over her classically knotted hair with the spray of delicate flowers, her pale green silk tabard and skirt. For a moment she was certain he was about to ask her to dance and her heartbeat quickened. Instead, he said, 'I must make the acquaintance of this rare creature.'

With that he excused himself and a few moments later, Ami saw him dancing with Joyce. After that, he danced with any number of appreciative women, some young, some old. He never did ask Ami to dance although she remained ready with a refusal all evening. It nettled her that she didn't have a chance to say no to him. And that, by staying away from her, he had managed to dominate her thoughts just as much as he would had he pursued her.

The bride threw her bouquet and it was caught by Sara Hardy, a local woman and writer who had found unexpected success with Emma's production of her first play. She plucked a single rose from the bouquet and tossed it back to the bride in thanks.

Emma and Matt flew away in his helicopter and the guests partied on for a while then gradually drifted home until only those guests staying overnight at Matt's homestead were left. After coffee, Ami went to bed, leaving the others drinking brandy and playing poker. North didn't even look up when she said good-night, just muttered a preoccupied, ''Night.' Which was fine by her. Just *fine*. Ami showered and slipped into a silk night shift, reflecting that she'd got accustomed to being pursued and this sudden change for the better took some adjusting to. The viral illness had left her more tired than usual and she drifted into a restless sleep dominated by dreams of scars and tight tuxedos.

CHAPTER EIGHT

She woke with a sudden thirst hours later and found the tumbler on her bedside table empty. Half asleep, she went into the adjacent bathroom to fill the glass, navigating her way by the moonlight flooding in from the uncurtained windows. When she came back, North was by her open bedroom door.

He was shouldered in against the doorframe, the picture of disreputable glamour—in need of a shave, his ruffled shirt open halfway down his chest, his bow tie hanging unknotted under his collar, traditional braces holding his borrowed pants a fraction too high. 'Beautiful Ami,' he said, crinkling his eyes. 'Can I have this dance?'

Her heart thudded. 'Are you drunk?' she said.

'Just a few brandies.' He looked appreciatively at the thin-strapped night shift, which only just covered her thighs. Ami went into her room, set down the water and snatched up her robe and when she looked back, North had stepped inside and closed the door.

'Everyone's gone to bed,' he said. 'Don't want to disturb them.' He put a finger ot his lips in the classic manner and she might have laughed except that his efforts not to disturb others so disturbed her. Pulling her wrap around herself she belted it tightly, as if she might suppress any response to this boyish, captivating Kendrick.

He eyed her bed, which was in the usual riotous tangle. By now he was well and truly aware that her rumpled sheets were routine, not the result of 'heavy nights.'

'It's nearly three in the morning. Why are you here?'

125

'To tell you we're driving back at nine tomorrow. Okay?'

She nodded.

North held out his hands. 'And to ask you to dance.'

She gave him a snort of impatience. 'It's a bit late for that. You should have asked me earlier, when the band was playing, but you were too busy being Mr Popularity.'

'I wanted to ask you to dance but—thought it best not to. Can't keep my distance if I'm holding you in my arms, can I?'

Her pulses thundered in her ears. 'Why, suddenly, do you want to keep your distance?'

'You're too much for me,' he said seriously. 'Better to stick to someone like Fran. I know Fran, understand her, understand what motivates her. Can't figure you out. Might never know what's underneath.' He reached out and drew a finger over her cheekbone, down to her chin, almost as if he expected the skin to peel off like a mask. 'Is this the real Ami Winterburn tonight? Looks like a temptress, acts like a severe nurse?'

'A temptress?' she snapped. Well, then, let him stick to Fran and that barren relationship, she thought in sudden rage. They could form a corporation. Poor Francesca, she thought in sudden sympathy.

He put a hand to her waist. 'Shall we waltz?' he said ironically. 'We waltz well together.'

His handprint was surely etched on to her skin. He's going to stick to Fran, she reminded herself. He still wants you but he's not going to chase you anymore. What, she wondered, had made North abandon the chase? But it was the conviction that he had that stopped her pulling away. It might be the last time he touched her. 'If I'm too much for you and you want to keep your distance, why ask me to dance now?'

North pulled her close, looked down at her affectionately. 'I'm drunk,' he explained, grinning.

She gave a shaky laugh but the laughter quickly died as he clasped her hand and hunched down, cheek to cheek, shuffling his feet in a parody of dancing. 'Mm,' he murmured, nuzzling her neck. 'Ami Winterburn,' he said, rolling her name out like the first line of a poem. He often said her full name like that, as if there was something else to come after it if he could just think of the next line.

Ami attempted to free herself, but she was half-hearted and in the process her arms slipped around his broad back and her mouth touched his neck and the scent of his skin assailed her. Ami closed her eyes. Just one cuddle while he was in this odd, boyish mood. Lucky Francesca, she thought, knifed by jealousy. They shuffled a few steps this way, then that, and suddenly North stopped. He looked at her, his hair falling over his forehead, and she saw the glitter of desire in his eyes.

'Ami Winterburn,' he whispered, laying a hand along the side of her face, and her name hung there, oddly unfinished, as he stroked downward, plucked the end of the silky belt and unravelled it. At his feather-light touch, the robe slithered from her shoulders. North held her close, bent his head to nuzzle in close, gathered up a handful of hair to expose her neck for his kiss. It was too much—the silken caress of his palm through her shift, the play of his fingers through her hair, the moist warmth of his mouth on her skin. He slipped the shift over her head, tossed it into the air and it fluttered in filmy slow motion to the floor. He drew back to look at her, naked now except for briefs. 'Beautiful Ami,' he said. In a new dance, they circled, locked in each other's gaze. Ami felt the edge of the bed behind her and sat down. North knelt and ran his hands over her in a delicate, tormenting exploration. 'Superb,' he said as he kissed her thigh. 'Magnificent—' he breathed, his head at her breasts. And Ami arched back, barely supporting herself as he suckled and fondled and pleasure rippled

through her body. A sigh broke from her. North laughed
softly and stood up to pull his shirt free of his waistband.
Moonlight threw shadows down one side of his body,
accentuating the hollow beneath his collarbone, the
sculptured curve of his chest and the small, neat nipples.
Her fingers tingled. Ami reached up and stroked the
junction of his neck and shoulder. North's eyes closed.
'Do that again when I have my hands free,' he said
huskily and hurried to get the cuff links from his shirt
sleeves. She stood and put her mouth to the same place
and he groaned and gave a delicate shiver, lifting his
shoulder into a defensive curve.

'How to make an angle into a curve,' she whispered
against his neck.

'Physics at a time like this?' he said huskily, doubling
his efforts. 'Damn all cuff links!'

Smiling, she let her fingers trail lower, to his waist.
North's chest heaved. Looking at him, seeing the expression of delicious strain on his face, she felt a heady
rush of power. She dipped lower still until she held him
in the palms of her hands.

He muttered something under his breath, ferociously
shook his shirt sleeves free. Laughing softly, she stretched
out on the bed and watched him in the moonlight, admiring the aesthetic lines of his shoulders and arms, an-
ticipating his strength, a lazy sensuality circulating in
her body. She heard the soft burr of a zip, the rustle of
his trousers, a clatter as a metal braces clip caught the
frame of the bed. Then the bed bounced under his weight
and she was in his arms, kissing him wildly, lost in a
starry space. He grasped her hips and tilted her evoca-
tively against him, an unnecessary action for she was
already breathless with the columned promise of the
beautiful, powerful body beneath her. North took some
deep breaths, which she rode in delicious anticipation.

'Ami,' he murmured. His strong hands were in her
hair, gathering it up with tenderness, forcing her eyelids

closed with the sheer hypnotic pleasure of the small caresses on her scalp. 'Is it safe?'

Safe. She rubbed her cheek against his hand, as
mindless and sensual as a cat. 'Safe for what?'

'For us to make love.'

She smiled. Sexy North Kendrick was also thoughtful
and responsible. She felt a surge of love for him. 'Yes.
Thank you for asking.' She kissed him passionately then
slid off the bed to step from her briefs, deliberately
slowing the moment, letting the anticipation build.

'Mm,' North groaned, watching her. He rolled on his
side and reached out to curve a hand to her thigh. 'Exquisite,' he said.

It was as if something switched in her head. She looked
down at him, saw the heavy-lidded look of the lover and
her body throbbed in response. But when he raised his
eyes to her face, she saw the glitter of triumph there.
And here she was, as frozen as one of the bronze torchbearers outside his hotel, with his hand on her in own-
ership. His fingertips moved gently on her skin as if he
was appreciating her flesh-and-blood smoothness the way
he'd appreciated the smoothness of the bronze.
Beautiful. Magnificent. Exquisite. She was almost part
of his collection. She reversed the direction of her briefs.
'Maybe I should be holding a torch,' she said, raising
her arm, striking a pose.

North stared at her, his spurned hand poised in a
frozen caress. 'A *torch*?'

'Or a sheaf of wheat or something,' she muttered. Ig-
noring the silk shift on the floor, she snatched up her
robe and turned her back to put it on. Was there anything more embarrassing than reclaiming in cold
soberness the clothes discarded in mindless passion? She
winced, switched on the bed lamp and gave herself a few
moments before she looked at North. He was hitched
up on one arm, his hair black as night, his long, mus-

cular body golden in the lamplight. Ami closed her eyes as her resolve weakened.

'Wheat?' he repeated carefully. 'You did say— *wheat*?'

'You're very good,' she said coolly.

His eyes narrowed. 'You stopped before you found out just how good.'

She flushed. 'You should be on the stage, North. You had me really believing in that boyish, affectionate persona.'

'Did I?' he said harshly.

'You aren't drunk. I daresay you've had a brandy or two but you're cold sober and as calculating as ever.'

North got up and put his hands on his hips. A formidable sight, almost naked as he was. His hands slanted down and inward like arrows and she turned away as her body mourned the pleasures she was rejecting.

'You do intend to enlighten me, I hope? I don't know what the hell you're talking about.'

'Oh, yes,' she said whirling around, picking up his clothes, her face burning as she remembered helping him off with his shirt, aiding and abetting him in her own acquisition. 'It was a good idea—a *great* idea. This is what you've been aiming for since the moment you decided you had to pay me back for humiliating you. You had to have me! Kendrick the Conqueror! All that rubbish about truces! Just Kendrick tactics like the charming little-boy-lost act—so appealing and frank because you've had too much brandy. Well, it didn't work!' she said, throwing his clothes at him.

North's head went back as he caught the bundle and the braces flicked at his face. His eyes looked cold as ice. 'It almost worked,' he said. To emphasize his point, he leaned down and picked up the silk shift, tossed it in the air, and its slow-motion descent created a time warp. Ami watched it, her mouth dry as the sight triggered a rush of desire.

'Like I said, you are very good at using your opportunities,' she snapped.

He shoved his arms into the sleeves of the frilled shirt and she thought she heard the sound of tearing stitches. 'I really must insist that I was—am—the worse for wear from too much brandy. Why would I be so stupid as to get mixed up with you again, otherwise?'

'So worse for wear that you could coolly check on—on—whether or not I—'

'On birth control arrangements?'

'I suppose you came with a prophylactic tucked away in your pocket!' she said contemptuously. 'Because you came here tonight with one purpose in mind.'

North pulled on his pants and snapped the zip. He looked at her with dislike. 'You don't know that. Even if it was true, you can't have it both ways. A man who doesn't give a damn is insensitive and irresponsible. A man who comes prepared is calculating.'

She blinked at the truth of that, knew she was being unfair but she had to persist because he was still here and in spite of everything she knew about him and the way he thought, she could so easily go to him and make love with him until morning, then wake up to find herself another exhibit in North's life. There was the staccato sound of a zip. The braces twanged.

At the door North looked again at the bed, which was now practically denuded of linen, the coverlet and top sheet flung in folds on the floor, the mattress cover showing. 'I'm afraid I've rumpled your sheets,' he drawled before he left.

Ami shut the door with a slam that brought muffled queries from other rooms and set Matt's cattle dogs barking. 'How could I?' Ami muttered as she remade the bed. 'Because I am an idiot!' Burning with self-censure, she got into bed to reflect upon her foolishness. But as the dogs quietened and the house fell silent once more, she reflected instead on what she would be doing

had North stayed. She would even now be in those strong
arms had she not come to her senses. She would be
stretched over his beautiful, hard body now if she had
not seen how degrading it all was. She would be holding
him inside her now, feeling the intimate flex of his
muscles, deliciously aware of the latent power in him as
he moved, just a little at first... If she had not seen
through North's games-playing in time. As the silent
morning hours passed she told herself it was a lucky thing
that she wasn't some young, foolish girl to fall for his
charm and expertise. Eventually she slept and dreamed
she was a young, foolish girl.

It was late morning by the time they arrived at Ken
Drummond's place in Swagman's Creek the following
day. After knocking fruitlessly at the front door, they
walked around the back of the small, timber house and
found Harry propped on his walking stick beside a
motorbike, the best-preserved of several dilapidated ve-
hicles that were scattered around the large, untidy al-
lotment on the edge of the tiny town. His old friend was
hunkered down beside him, pointing out something with
the zeal of the enthusiast. Spritz came bounding towards
them, as pleased to see North, Ami thought resentfully,
as the owner who lovingly fed and groomed her.

North came to a halt, watching his father. He wore
sunglasses as he had during the journey and Ami could
only guess that the degree of frost in his eyes paralleled
that in his voice. North was either genuinely offended
by her accusations last night, or just a bad loser. She
opted for the latter. His mood improved with Spritz's
unqualified adoration, but dissipated quickly when
Harry greeted them.

'Driving back with us?' Harry said eagerly to Ami.
She shook her head.

'My car is ready. I'm driving back just as soon as I
pick it up.'

Harry was clearly disappointed. 'In that case, maybe it would be better if I waited and drove back with Ami,' he said undiplomatically to his son. Harry couldn't make it clearer that he preferred her company to that of his son on the long drive back to Sydney.

North's jaw tightened and Ami would have left then except that Harry's bachelor friend pointed with sheepish pride to a ramshackle outdoor table set with four mismatched teacups, a pint jug of milk, a plate of thick fruitcake slices and a tin of biscuits. 'Don't often have company,' he said, pink-faced, to explain such an elaborate table. 'I'll bring the teapot.'

He duly brought it and went back to contemplate the bike with the other two men. Ami sighed, realizing that she had been assigned to pour the tea as a natural consequence of being the only female present. As she did so, the motorbike started up with an ancient shriek. To her surprise, she saw North was riding it, skillfully dodging the various back yard obstacles, including a sheep that placidly cropped grass in the midday shade of a row of camphor laurel trees that stretched to the back boundary. Harry and Ken absently took the tea she handed them, watching North's progress with the kind of attention and approval only males can give such an activity. On Harry's face was also a look of deep envy. He grimaced at Ami. 'I'd give a lot to get on a bike again, but my legs—' he said wistfully.

North, his black mood considerably reduced by the ride, throttled down and parked and the three men had an earnest exchange based on the sound of the revs. Ami stared at North, the usually immaculate company director and art collector who was now crouched down, sunglasses off, pointing out something in a rusting old heap of machinery that emitted an unearthly sound. The noise would be horrendous to a man who really had imbibed too much brandy the night before, she thought, unable to detect the slightest flicker of his eyelids. Harry ran a fond hand over the bike handles and the fairing and, following the movement, North said, 'Whatever happened to your bikes, Harry?'

'I've still got one. It's in my shed. Was always going to fix it but it'll never run again,' he said flatly. 'I gave the others away.'

Harry, Ami thought, had given a lot of things away. North looked thoughtful and the three men stood in a circle, arms folded, united in the mysterious masculine passion for machinery. Ami took advantage of their pre-occupation to leave before she was dragged into a fight between North and his father about the journey back. She left a note on the table to say that she was walking to the garage to pick up her car, took her suitcase from the Jaguar and set off up the road with Spritz beside her. The drone of the motorbike made her look back. Beyond the stripe of the camphor laurels' dense blue shade, the rough ground of Ken's paddock was a hazy yellow in the sun. She caught a glimpse of the bike in the bright spaces between the trees until it emerged into the open. Ami laughed.

'Oh, Spritz, look at that,' she said, shading her eyes. She thought of that photograph of a young North, his face showing anxiety and pleasure and pride, riding pillion behind Harry all those years ago. Now it was North with Harry behind him, holding on, making good his wish to get on a bike again. Unseen, she stood and watched until the bike turned and flickered from view behind the line of trees.

Ami walked on down the lane, her eyes watering. Why did it matter to her whether North made peace with his father? Why on earth should she feel this flutter of anxiety lest he make a mess of what might be a tentative reconciliation? Because she cared. 'Oh, you *stupid*!' she said out loud, kicking a twig off the road as if she was kicking North out of her mind. Spritz pounced on it and brought it back to her. Ami tossed it into the scrub at the side of the lane. Half fallen was a retrievable position. It had to be true. She couldn't face the prospect of falling in love with a man who liked his champagne cold and his women beautiful. The dusty lane stretched out ahead. The sunlight limned tall seed heads in the waist-high grass along. the road. The sound of the motorbike followed her in fits and starts like the sound of an exuberant insect on the still, country air.

Spritz brought the stick back again and again and insisted on taking it into the car. It was still in the car when they reached Sydney where she tossed it out. Out of sight, out of mind. Unfortunately the same could not be said for North.

North himself phoned her on the Friday following Emma's wedding.

'Ami,' he said briskly. 'I haven't got much time. Can you come over to the hotel?'

She felt the usual dual irritation and excitement at his voice and the prospect of seeing him again. 'I haven't got much time, either,' she said coolly. 'What is it about? Is Harry all right?'

'He's fine,' he said impatiently. 'I can't go into it on the phone. How long will it take you to get here? Half an hour—forty-five minutes?'

'Just a minute! I'm not going to drop everything—'

'And don't make any plans for this weekend,' he said.

She took a deep, deep breath. Adrenalin pumped into her system. 'The weekend?' The ragged nature of her heartbeat aggravated her. 'Look,' she said, opting for anger rather than this weak-kneed speculation. 'My weekends are none of your business.'

'This one will be,' he said smoothly. 'I'm calling in a favour, Ami Winterburn. And if you don't like it, too bad. You shouldn't start things you don't intend to finish.' He gave her a moment to digest that and added, 'If you set out now, you can be here in forty minutes.'

She bridled at the gall of it. 'And I suppose if I don't I can expect a letter from your lawyers?'

She thought she heard him swear under his breath but when he spoke, his voice was silkily earnest. 'I would hate to implicate your partner in the irresponsible hoax that was, after all, exclusively *your* idea, but—'

'All *right*,' she snapped. 'You really are the lowest—'

But North had rung off.

The threat was possibly a bluff but she wasn't sure enough of him to call it. Even if things had improved with his father, his mood would be anything but benign where she was concerned. It would not be often that North was rejected in the middle of lovemaking. In the middle of his best-laid plans.

Almost-laid plans.

Her face flamed as precise images from that night presented themselves yet again to her. She had let him take her in his arms against her better judgment. She had danced with him in her bedroom when she'd planned all along to refuse, when she *should* have refused. She'd sprawled on the bed, ogled him. She'd caressed him, held him in the most intimate way... her fingers tingled. She drifted off for a few hectic moments.

How unfortunate the timing had been. Every year when Emma and Matt celebrated their wedding anniversary, she would be forced to remember her folly with North in the west. She gave a wry laugh.

The memory triggers were mounting up. The waltz from *Rosenkavalier* could set her thinking about North. The fragrance of a gardenia. Her best friend's wedding date. The dog. Motorbikes. Santa Claus suits. Viruses. Cheap checkered shirts. The kitchen sink...

As she drove to the hotel, she dissected his words, read between the lines. *You shouldn't start things you don't intend to finish.* A deep foreboding filled her. What if he wanted to finish what she had started that night?

No, surely not. Manipulation and blackmail might be in the Kendrick genes, but she couldn't see North demanding sexual favours in exchange for amnesty over her masquerade as Amelia.

Still, she sailed past the torchbearers with a distracted air. She nearly missed seeing the tall woman in the tight, black leggings and the blue sweater with alphabet letters printed on the front. But she turned at the Avalon doors and saw the blonde approach a man, with an unlit cigarette between her extended fingers. Ami saw her lips move in the classic words, 'Got a light?'

So that was her doppelgänger, she thought. It did nothing to endear her to North, knowing that she did loosely fit the description on his security records. Even if she *had* turned out to be the woman on the street, he had no business being so patronising, so downright arrogant on the day of the gardenia. Ami felt like warning the woman that she was probably even now under surveillance, but when she looked again, she had disappeared. The hawk-eyed Morgan, she saw, as she passed through the doors, had not noticed the woman, which gave her spirits a curious little lift.

The concierge sent her to the floor below North's penthouse. 'You'll find Mr. Kendrick in the Celestial Suite.'

The door was ajar and Ami went in. North was standing by a glass wall that overlooked a breathtaking view of Sydney seen through swathes of sheer fabric. He was on the phone and turned around when she entered. He waved her towards the lushly upholstered armchairs. Ami was forced to cool her heels while he continued his call and she thought bitterly how very well he used the tools of technology to give himself an advantage. She paced the length of the room, which was furnished rather floridly with divans and chairs covered in mauve and turquoise brocade with tasselled cushions. On low tables stood huge oriental jars filled with tiger lilies, strelitzia and jasmine, the origin of the perfume in the air. The lavish interior hinted more of earthly than celestial matters. All it needed was a sheikh and a dancing girl with a diamond in her navel. Her eyes flicked from the lush fabrics to the frankly sexual tiger lilies to North himself. His eyes followed her every move. What did he want? What did he mean—*you shouldn't start things you don't mean to finish*?

He put the phone down and her muscles tensed as he studied each small detail of her appearance. If he took as much interest in the inner woman as he did in the outer, she thought prudishly, he would be a prince among men. He wore one of his superb three-piece suits with a blue shirt that tinged his grey eyes with its colour.

'You took off rather suddenly from Ken's place,' he said. 'I would have driven you to the garage eventually.'

'What's this about, North? What is this *favour* I owe you? If it's payment you want for nursing me through a viral illness, then I'd prefer to write you a cheque for your time.'

There was a pause, during which Ami realized just how insulting that sounded, even to someone like North, who thought the world operated on those terms. His eyes glittered. 'No, no,' he said in that silky voice that filled her with misgivings. 'I feel you repaid that debt the night of the wedding. Perhaps not quite in *full*—' He gave a wolfish smile, as if remembering how close to full payment she had been. 'I'm still puzzling over your reference to a sheaf of wheat. It was wheat? Do you have a cereal fetish, or something?'

Flushed, Ami looked at him with dislike and suspicion. 'I'm very busy. What do you want?'

'Like I said, I'm calling in a favour—you owe me, Ami Winterburn...' As usual, her name did not quite finish the sentence. But there was no more to come save a very explicit scrutiny that made her wonder if the room was unseasonably heated.

'How do you like your suite?' he said at last.

'Ami stared around at the opulent interior. '*My* suite?'

'Yours,' he confirmed, watching her the way a cat watches a mouse.

'What are you talking about?'

'I—feel I want you near,' he said, walking around her, looking her over. 'So that we can finish this business once and for all. I'll be here in Sydney over the weekend and it would be—*convenient* if you were handy.'

'*Convenient*!' A pulse hammered in her temple.

'I'm a generous man. I've even provided a new wardrobe for you to use while you're, er, staying with me.'

'You *can't* think what I think you mean!'

'You once asked what would satisfy me,' he murmured. 'You can't be so naive not to know the answer.'

She felt a shaming little thrill that made her cut the air contemptuously with the edge of her hand. 'Forget it. I'd dive into a tankful of sharks before I'd go to bed with you.'

His brows went up in mock surprise at such plain speaking. 'I suppose that explains that little interlude we shared after Emma's wedding,' he said blandly. 'You couldn't find a tankful of sharks? Scarce in the outback.'

'Very amusing,' she snapped, feeling a furnace heat in her cheeks.

'You made a fool of me, Ami Winterburn. I didn't like that.'

Ami tried to read the conflicting messages in his eyes but was defeated by a recollection of him in his underwear, by lamplight—the frustrated, baffled lover. She felt some vague pangs of guilt in spite of her knowledge of his devious behaviour.

'I have to—how did you put it? Restore my self-esteem. All I want is your—company, for a short time. To, um, finish the affair properly,' he said with a look so wolfish it just had to be fake. She frowned at him, suddenly realizing that her intuition was telling her there was something wrong here. But his expression grew so smug that her normal thought processes were blocked by anger.

'Come, take a look at the clothes I've bought for you,' he said, showing his teeth, and she abandoned her battling intuition. She was still trapped in that dangerous habit women had, she thought in self-disgust—trying hard to believe that no matter how manipulative and selfish a man was, he couldn't be all bad.

North walked through an adjoining door wondering if sheer curiosity would make her follow him. It did. He smiled as he heard the outraged rustle of her clothes behind him. There were massive jardinières here, full of exotic orchids in the fleshy pinks and decadent purples the decorators deemed correct for this most bordello-like suite in the hotel. There was an enormous, cushioned bed on a dais, silk-draped from the ceiling. Tassels everywhere. North mounted the dais and delicately tested the mattress with spread fingertips. Pure corn, he thought, glancing over to see if she had twigged yet.

She was clearly torn between fury and a hysterical desire to laugh. But her normal very reliable sense of the ridiculous was being suppressed by some other strong feeling and she fell for it. North was elated. He still had some old scores to settle with Ami Winterburn.

'You *can't* be serious?' she said scathingly.

'Being serious is a failing of mine,' he said. 'I'm sure you recall Harry pointing that out. Here's the wardrobe.'

At his touch, large carved doors opened to reveal some clothes still wearing the maker's tags.

'I can't believe even *you* would be so crass as to—to proposition one woman while you're on the brink of marriage to another.'

He blinked a bit at that, not aware that he was on the brink of marriage but quite prepared to play along with it. 'But as you've remarked in the past, I never waste an opportunity,' he said dryly, thinking of that night that was so frustratingly hazy when he tried to remember just how it had felt to have her naked in his arms, yet so painfully clear when it came to her denouncement afterwards. He took out a garment and arranged it over his forearm, as if he was an old-fashioned draper, inviting her approval.

She did hesitate for a moment then, as if she was picking up the clues but something was interfering with her judgment. The confident, articulate Miss Winterburn was red-faced, her magnificent breasts were heaving as she grabbed the dress and flung it on the floor. 'Keep your harem clothes for some other—' The fallen garment caught her eye at last. Powder blue linen. Long sleeves, buttoned at the wrist. Tiny pearl buttons up to the neck. Neat collar with guipure lace.

She spun around to the wardrobe, riffled through the clothes. North grinned when her straight back stiffened as she got a closer look at the harem clothes. A dove-grey dress and jacket. A pleated skirt, a matronly blouse and cashmere cardigan. Refined clothes for the older woman. Monica from the executive gifts service hadn't turned a hair when he'd given a description and estimated vital statistics of the widow Anderson.

Ami seized a pair of shoes from a shelf. Her size, but high-cut, lace-ups with sensible heels.

'Built in arch supports,' North said helpfully, pointing over her shoulder. 'So essential for legs that have been through so much.' He smiled fondly at her. 'Amelia.'

She swallowed, put a hand to her forehead as she finally twigged. Miss Winterurn was very slow on the uptake today, which meant that whatever was on her mind was something very weighty indeed. North found it a source of great optimism.

'You mean—stay here as Amelia *Anderson*?'

'My favourite old lady. I invited her to stay, free of charge, remember?'

CHAPTER NINE

SHE had forgotten all about Amelia Anderson, had lost her cool entirely and plunged headlong into assumptions that might be all too revealing. Ami closed her eyes briefly, winced at the echo of her babble about sharks and harems. She had come here with her thoughts firmly stuck in that time warp, the night of Emma's wedding when they'd started something and hadn't finished it. With luck, he would get so much enjoyment out of making an idiot of her that he wouldn't notice.

'I've been pestered by reporters wanting to follow up on the heart-warming story of the elderly gatecrasher having her free holiday in the Avalon. I've managed to put them off with excuses until now. You'll be interested to know that since she gatecrashed my party, Amelia has had a nasty bout of flu and has been to visit her son in New Zealand—or was it Canada?'

She glowered, not trusting herself to speak.

'Somehow I assumed they would lose interest in the widow but it's nearly Christmas and you know how the papers love human interest stories in the season of goodwill.'

'But it's a risk,' she said, aghast. 'What if I'm sprung this time?'

'This isn't like you, Miss Winterburn,' he chided, giving her a hearty slap on the back. 'Where is all that immodest confidence in your skill? Besides, I'm not giving you a choice. How would it look if I can't produce the widow Anderson cosily enjoying the holiday I promised her? Some nosy reporter might run a check on social security and discover there is no Amelia Anderson.

143

There are only two conclusions that could be reached from that—one, that I was properly fooled, or, two, that I knew about the impersonation and knowingly made idiots of my guests and the press. I,' he told her softly, 'have no intention of being labelled either fool or cheat. You've been successful in audition at last, Miss Winterburn,' he said maliciously. 'The part of Amelia Anderson is yours. Playing this weekend by popular request.'

She stared. So that's what he meant by finishing what she'd started. To finish the affair properly, he'd said. The affair of Amelia Anderson. The affair of the gardenia. There was a certain crazy logic to it, she supposed. She could once and for all allay those feelings of guilt she had over the impersonation. Make up for witnessing his humiliation, give Harry one last thrill but this time with his son in on the joke, which would help to paper over the rough edges between the two men. Rather than a tedious, unsatisfying fade-out, a definite event to mark THE END. It appealed to Ami's sense of drama. Amelia's swan song would be hers, too. She swallowed.

'Surely not the entire weekend,' she objected. 'It would only take an hour for a press photographer to take some shots.'

'Two press photographers,' he corrected. 'One on Saturday night, one on Sunday sometime. You'll stay overnight and make yourself seen around the hotel. Several guests have enquired about dear old Amelia. You have tugged at so many heartstrings.'

'And what am I supposed to do about Spritz?'

'I'll spring for the cost of a kennel—which is more than fair in the circumstances,' he said. 'After all, *I* did not create the widow Anderson.'

'You could have simply *told* me the press were being a nuisance,' she said, with a sigh. 'I do have some sense of responsibility, you know. I don't have to be coerced into helping in a situation I helped create.'

'I know that,' he said, amused. 'But you have such a poor opinion of me—I couldn't resist stringing you along when I saw your suspicions written all over you.'

She snorted. 'Childish.'

'Put it down to my atrophied sense of humour,' he said ironically and she saw with surprise that Harry's criticism still stung. He bent to pick the blue linen dress from the floor. Flicking her a wicked glance, he shook it, slipped it on the hanger and put it away. Ami had to press her lips together to hold back a laugh at the recollection of herself, flinging it to the floor as if it was a black lace negligee with strings attached.

'You made quite a few assumptions there,' he commented, touching a long spike of orchids. The flowers trembled and he plucked one, casually raised it to his nose as they walked out to the sitting room. 'Jumped to conclusions that I'd inveigled you here to force you into bed with me.' He paused, looked expectantly at her but she refused to bite. 'Psychologically speaking, we tend to make assumptions based on what we *fear* might happen, or on what we *want* to happen. Which was it in this case—maybe a bit of both?'

'Maybe you should apply that theory to some of your own assumptions, North,' she retorted. 'You've jumped to conclusions almost every time you've met me. And every time they've led you to want to throw me out.' She paused alongside him, looked mockingly at him. 'Psychologically speaking, we tend to want to exclude things that frighten us, or are too complex for us to deal with. What was it in my case, North? Maybe a combination of both?'

'Touché,' he murmured, staring into her eyes.

It irritated her, that polite, sportsmanlike acknowledgment of a point scored—the kind of graciousness extended by champions who knew they would win in the end anyway and could afford to be generous. But the spurt of irritation was not enough to set her feet moving. Her heightened senses picked up a heady drift of jasmine, the faint, rising sounds of the city through the open terrace doors, the tremor of the breeze in the sheer, swathed curtains. She stood there, held in some mysterious communication that was changing nature second by second. Puzzled, she sought to describe it, but it seemed independent of any words they had exchanged. In his grey eyes she saw the same faint surprise, followed by acceptance. A pleasant warmth came to her, and the magnetic pull of attraction. North, she thought, as if it was on a map. A direction. A destination. Magnetic North.

They moved at the same time, heads tilted until their lips met. A scarce, tender touch as if they were teenagers and it was their first kiss. North sighed and she felt the warm rush of his breath in her mouth. Again they kissed, leisurely, equally open one to the other. There was no other point of contact between them, just mouth on mouth, tongue speaking direct to tongue with no distractions. Language seemed obsolete. There was simply this tender, electrifying, intense communication on some level Ami had never before encountered. In perfect synchronisation, they moved apart again, seeing the shaken realization in each other's eyes, that something new had happened, something that transcended anything that went before. Ami's chest felt tight, emotion welled up in her and for a moment she thought she might cry at the puzzling sense of something beautiful and elusive.

North saved her from anything so foolish. He broke the contact, leaned over and tucked the orchid into her hair.

'I won't throw you out this weekend,' he said, giving her face a little pat.

So much for a mysterious, mutual communication, she thought, deriding herself. So much for tran-

scendence and recognition and some elevated level of
transmission between two people. It was all skill and
technique for North and it was all wishful thinking on
her part to imagine it was anything else.

It was only when she got back to the shop that she
realized why so many people had stared at her along the
way. North's orchid was still tucked behind her ear,
marking his place. Once again she removed it too late
and was only prevented from throwing it out by Helen,
who never got orchids and, scandalised by the waste,
snatched it to the safety of a water glass where it mocked
Ami for the remainder of the day.

Ami duly made her appearances in the hotel on
Saturday afternoon, to give credence to the idea that
Amelia Anderson was a guest. Accompanied by North,
she drank coffee in the coffee shop where he had his
revenge by insisting on an in-depth discussion of lamp-
shade making which tested her powers of invention. She
visited the indoor pool and was introduced to several
guests by a solicitous North who watched her performance critically with the satisfaction of one who was
in on the joke at last. On Saturday evening, when her
skin was itching from the long contact with adhesive,
she posed for a number of shots, ending up in the restaurant, where the newspaper photographer took shots
of the pensioner being wined and dined by the benevolent entrepreneur. The entire business had the
hallmark of North's organization upon it. It was he who
decided where she would be photographed, to ensure the
best possible conditions for deception, and for once she
was pleased that his high-handedness invited no argument from the cameraman. A reporter turned up and
Ami had reason to be grateful again, this time for the
semiinvisibility of an old woman, even one supposedly
in the limelight. North hardly let her say a word and the
young male reporter didn't find it odd at all, that a man

was running the show and spoke on behalf of a woman twice his age.

Because of the interest generated amongst other patrons, North insisted that they sit through the remainder of dinner after the press had gone, when Ami was breaking her neck to escape to her room and take off her make-up. He was expansive and complacent and she glared at him.

'Wouldn't you rather we skipped dessert?' she said primly. 'I'm sure you'd prefer to spend time with Francesca on a Saturday night.'

He laughed and took her hand, patting it kindly. 'It's you I want to be with Amelia, honestly.' He took her hand and lightly bestowed a kiss on the made-up surface.

'The warm and human side of big business,' she said sardonically under her breath. 'The very important North Kendrick being nice to an impoverished, elderly nobody.'

There was a gleam of anger in his grey eyes as he paused, her hand still raised in his. He turned her hand over. 'The very irritated, besotted North Kendrick trying to find a chink in the armour of the infuriating, desirable Ami Winterburn...' he murmured. Eyes never leaving hers, he put his mouth to her palm, the only available part of her that was not defended by disguise. The warm caress of his lips sent a frisson down her back. She jumped at the sly touch of his tongue.

Besotted? she thought, staring into those silvery-grey eyes.

'Did you say—' she began, when Franesca showed up, elegant in black with a tiger-skin-patterned silk scarf thrown about her neck, its ends floating to her knees.

Francesca said a polite hello to the widow Anderson, averting her eyes quickly from the threatening vision of age and wrinkles. 'You've been simply ages,' she said to North, an excited light in her lovely eyes. 'I'm dying to talk to you.'

Besotted, Ami thought derisively, as they left the restaurant. Of course he hadn't said besotted. Or if he had, it was an ironic turn of phrase.

Gloomily she tried to achieve some professional satisfaction at carrying out yet another performance without giving the game away. One more performance the following day and the affair would be finished once and for all. But her mind was on North and Francesca, who had disappeared, arms linked, having escorted Ami to her room. By now they were probably on their way to some intimate little place where they could dance cheek to cheek ... and Francesca could whisper in North's ear whatever it was she was dying to tell him.

Harry phoned her when she had finally cleansed her face and let the skin breathe. 'Come on up and have a drink with me,' he said.

But when she got to the penthouse she found that North and Francesca were not in any cosy little restaurant, they were here with Harry.

Francesca looked at Ami in puzzlement when no-one introduced her to the stranger. 'I thought you said Mrs. Anderson was coming up to stay a while with you, Harry?'

The old man gave a wheezy laugh. 'Oh, this is her, er, goddaughter, Ami,' he said at last.

'The fairy goddaughter,' North murmured, a gleam in his eyes.

They left and Ami stayed for an hour in North's home, vowing never to come here again. As she talked to Harry, her eye was drawn from one work of art to another—paintings, sculptures, the ancient Grecian pots in their lit display dome. How long would North keep these, she wondered, before his enthusiasm waned? Besotted one minute, indifferent the next. Poor Francesca.

Back in her suite she was so restless she knew she wouldn't sleep. It was after eleven when she changed into the leotard and tights she had packed, put on some battered practice dance shoes and attempted a work-out. She gave up in frustration, for the suite, though spacious, was not nearly spacious enough to give vent to her feelings. She would need a space the size of a ballroom to do that tonight.

A ballroom.

Ami's heartbeat quickened. She visualised that vast space. It was probably hired out for a wedding or twenty-first birthday party, crowded with tables and chairs and guests. But it would do no harm to look. She pulled on a long sweater over her tights, cinched her hair into a ponytail and made her way to the Avalon ballroom. It was empty save for clustered tables, a lectern and stacked chairs at one end left over from a conference.

She found a switch, turned on some recessed lighting, which shed a candle-like glow along the mirrored side of the huge room. Using one of the chairs as a *barre*, she warmed up with some exercises. Then she removed her sweater and progressed to centre practice, slow, fluid movements, then small jumps. The shiny expanse all around her went to her head and she moved into quicker movements, travelling the length of the ballroom in a series of leaps and turns, her feet making soft, rhythmic thuds on the floor, her image flickering alongside in the mirror. She stopped at last for a breather and warm-down, one leg raised on the back of a chair, her head thrown back. And she saw the other image in the mirror.

North. Her heartbeat, slowing already after the workout, bumped into reverse. The sound of her breathing seemed abnormally loud as she looked at him in the mirror, wondering if she had gone right off the rails now and was conjuring up his image like a fey ballet heroine languishing over her imagined prince. Music started up, in her head or in reality she wasn't sure.

'It's after midnight,' he said, removing any doubt of his earthly nature. The sound of his shoes, measured on the fine parquetry flooring, kept time with the boom of her heartbeat. 'I thought fairy goddaughters were supposed to turn into pumpkins at midnight.' Closer now, his gaze dripped warmly down over her body.

Supremely aware of him, she continued her warm-down exercises to the music that was, she realized, coming from the hidden speakers. It was the tail end of something by one of the Strausses and it concluded with a rousing blast before silence fell. 'I hope you don't mind me using the ballroom,' she said huskily.

'I saw you dance. You take my breath away.'

He'd taken hers. Ami stared at him, while on the edge of her vision she could make out his image and hers in the mirror, facing each other motionless like two inhabitants of a Degas painting. She with a leg raised and outstretched, one foot still resting on the back of a chair, he with an arm outstretched to the same resting place, his hand beside her foot. The music started again, the first celebratory whoops of orchestra brass followed by strings as the music swelled from the introduction into the waltz from *Der Rosenkavalier*. There were words to this music, she thought. Something about the night being too long . . .

'They're playing our song, Ami Winterburn . . .'

Some part of her listened for the unsaid words following her name, but there was only the music.

'Dance with me,' he said.

She'd meant not to dance with him the last time. There were more reasons than ever to refuse now. Reason number one—look what happened last time. Reason number two—if she kept clear of North, she would be finished with this affair in a matter of hours. Reason number three—she was more than half in love with him, but he was still the wrong kind of man for her. Four—Francesca. Five—*look what happened last time*. Six—*Francesca* . . .

'What about Francesca?' she said abruptly.

'She doesn't want to dance with me.'

'How do you know?'

'She told me tonight. Doesn't want to dance with me, ever,' he said, placing his hand firmly on her ankle. Ami drew in a sharp breath at that imprisoning, pleasant grip. 'She said she thought I was a sexy brute but she couldn't ever fall in love with me.'

'That's what she was dying to tell you?'

'That's it, broadly speaking.'

'But you were going to marry her, always supposing she would have you,' she said dryly.

'I might have considered it, in my ignorance, before—'

Before what? She waited but he didn't finish it. It was a habit with him, she thought, those unfinished sentences. He had been going to stick with Fran. Whether he would have or not was purely academic because Fran was not going to stick with him. This was nothing to celebrate, she told herself as her heartbeat sped up. This made no difference to her. He was still the kind of man who could contemplate such a lukewarm but convenient partnership. The man who liked his women beautiful, his champagne cold and his collector's items new and fresh. He would find another Francesca in time. But he was here now, his touch warm on her body, and her blood pounded in her veins and the tempo of the waltz was inside her. How did the words go? *Something, something, keine nacht ist zu lang*. The night was too long? She struggled with her schoolgirl German to translate. *Something, something, no night is too long*.

Impatiently, he dragged the chair aside, removing the barrier between them with a rasp of chair legs on the polished floor. Then he caught her close to him and they waited there a moment staring into each other's eyes while the music slowed to one of those breathless pauses when every nerve in the body anticipated the resumption of the sound. When it came, they went with it, slowly at first, locked together, intent on each other, hardly admitting the music. But as the rhythm quickened, they spun to the exuberant rhythm. This time Ami wasn't pretending to be anyone else, wasn't pretending anything at all. The ballroom whirled by, a blur of light and shadow, the only constant North himself, smiling, holding her fast in a dizzy world. *With you, with you, no night is too long.* I love you, she thought, feeling the forbidden words bubble to the surface, not quite spoken. The music slowed and released them, breathless and exhilarated.

'I wondered what it would be like to dance like that with you, that night when you waltzed me around cautiously as if I might break.' Ami threw back her head and laughed and North caught in a deep breath, hauling her hard against him.

'I don't think I can be cautious tonight. Will you break?'

His eyes glittered, his nostrils gently flared and she felt a rush of desire, a heightened sense of danger and aliveness. Like teetering on a high, narrow ledge, the risk of losing life making life more intense.

'What would you do if I did?'

North put his mouth to her ear. She could feel his smile on her skin. 'I'd mend you,' he murmured, suturing an imaginary line along her neck with a series of kisses and flicks of the tongue that made her gasp out his name.

She felt the jolt of his response to her ragged cry. He crushed her in his arms, kissed her mouth, hotly forging an entrance, filling her mouth with the taste of him. Stooping, he picked her up bodily and walked from the ballroom, his mouth on hers, her arms wrapped around his shoulders.

'Let me down,' she said indistinctly as they stopped by the lift and he punched a button with his elbow. 'Someone might see.'

'I don't give a damn if they do,' he growled. He jabbed the button. 'What's taking the damned lift so long?'

'Am I getting too heavy?' she said innocently, taking a nibble at his ear lobe.

He gave her a look so warm that she wondered if her hair was singed. 'No. But if the elevator doesn't come soon, I might make love to you here on the floor.'

And so in tune with him was she that the prospect was hardly shocking at all. But the lift came and by the time they were inside Ami's suite, her hair was streaming loose and North's shirt was unbuttoned beneath his jacket and his tie hung over his beautiful bare chest. North set her down and his hands roved the resistant, seamless Lycra dance gear and his urgent, escalating efforts to remove it sent shivers of delight and apprehension through her body. He was so strong, so passionate, so impatient and she suddenly panicked as his will carried her too fast, too soon. Whether or not he sensed something, he paused, his hands stilled, defeated by the impenetrable, skin-tight Lycra.

'Ami Winterburn...still encased in armour,' he said huskily, holding her at arm's length suddenly. He took several deep breaths and curbed his ferocity. Ami saw the gleam in his eyes as he forced himself back from the brink. Her mouth went dry. If there was anything more guaranteed to raise her temperature than North impatient to make love, it was North disciplining himself to match her pace. Making himself wait. She smiled, dazzled by him.

'I could make love to you now, this moment, anywhere, I don't care.' He took her hand, raised it to his mouth. 'But I want to make it last...'

He made it last and so did she, for how long she couldn't say. A tender, mutual exploration that set her senses reeling, made her wonder if she'd ever known what it was like to be really alive outside his arms. North was a lover to cherish, she already knew that. A strong, vigorous lover who kept his power in check, making it all the more exciting. She stood before him as she shed the tights and North took a long, long time to smooth her underwear from her with lingering, seductive strokes down her thighs and calves. He pulled her along with him and sat on a divan, spinning her at the last moment so that she sprawled on his lap, her back against his bare chest, her head dropped back into the mellow curve of his neck in a pose of sheer abandonment. And if she thought she had been aroused before, she found now that there were higher planes of arousal and higher still as North played her body like an instrument, his hard heat behind her, his fingers moving over her skin, fondling, finding all the secret parts of her. 'North,' she cried raggedly, urgently.

'North it is,' he murmured in her ear and moved his hands northwards to her breasts, where he produced sensations that kept her on a plateau of pleasure with the promise of high mountains and an endless sky. And just when she thought she might make the journey alone, he turned her to face him and she wrapped her long legs around him and he spread his hands over her hips and looked deep in her eyes. 'Ami Winterburn,' he said softly, lowering her to him, inch by tormenting inch. Her eyes almost closed with pleasure but she forced them open, watching North's flickering lashes, the glaze in his eyes, the flush high on his cheeks as he entered her. She kissed him, filled with love and a peculiar joy she'd never experienced. Locked together in intimacy, they were still, her head on his shoulder, his arms close around her. Every nerve in her body tingled with anticipation, waiting for the music to resume. And when it started, it ran away with them, faster and faster. Through the window behind North, the glittering city was a mass of shifting light points—stars slipping from their places in the sky. Her mouth was against his forehead, her arms close around the rippling muscles of his back, and she thought she

might have called out something about love when she
left the glorious plateau for the mountains and then the
sky, the great, glittering, immense sky that went on
forever . . .

Later, smiling, they stretched out on the divan with
its cushions scattered to the four winds in testimony to
their activities. They wore the towelling robes provided
by the hotel and sipped at coffee made by Ami. She
flushed, gradually growing self-conscious as North's eyes
roamed over her, his intimate knowledge of her making
them warm and lazy. The heat of passion began to seem
just a tiny bit silly as her head cooled. 'That was—' she
began, and bit her lip.

'What?' North prompted, lifting a heavy swathe of
hair from her face with an index finger. 'Good, bad,
indifferent?'

His grin was so complacent that she was peeved. No
doubts for North Kendrick. No lingering little worries
that he might not have been a satisfactory lover. She'd
left him in no doubt with her moans and cries. There
were even the marks of her fingernails visible on that
juncture of his neck and shoulder exposed by his loosely
tied robe. Ami averted her eyes from them, irked that
she had left the visible signs of her pleasure for him or
anyone else to see. Red-faced, she said rather more
sharply than she intended, 'I suppose I should be glad
we made it as far as the divan. You did talk about
throwing me down in the corridor . . .' Her colour
deepened at the idea that hadn't turned a hair of her
head when she'd been in the throes of desire.

North looked at her with great interest. 'Was it a bit
too unconventional for you, Ami?'

'Yes. No! I mean—oh!' she said crossly, pulling the
edges of the robe primly over her knees, a move that
amused North no end. What on earth did she do now?
Would he get up and leave? Thanks for the coffee. See
you in the morning. It wasn't as if she'd never had a

lover, but this was North and she was already dying of embarrassment. It made her acerbic. 'It just seems more—civilised to use a bedroom,' she said, scowling.

'You're embarrassed,' he said softly.

'Not at all.'

'Ami Winterburn...' he said, smoothing her hair again, and she thought for a moment he was going to add something to her name. 'Fearless Ami, embarrassed by her own fervour.'

'Fervour?' she said, attempting nonchalance in vain.

'You are a tigress,' he said, growling in the back of his throat.

'An embarrassed tigress? Isn't that rather unlikely?'

'You are a woman of great contradictions. This coffee is good.'

'Does that surprise you?'

'Not at all. It's hard to go wrong with instant coffee,' he said equably.

She glared at him. 'I meant—that I'm a person of contradictions?'

'Nothing about you could surprise me anymore,' he said, putting down his coffee cup. He rose, took her hand and pulled her to her feet. Ami's heart began a heavy, pounding beat as she found herself in the circle of his arms, his mouth lightly on her temple. Taking her by the hand, he set off across the room.

'What are you doing?' she said.

North smiled wickedly at her. 'I've got this sudden craving to be conventional,' he told her as he tugged her into the bedroom with its silk-draped bed on a dais. She stared at him as her body revved into high gear again. His towelling robe gaped to the waist, showing large tracts of very desirable man. His eyes had the sheen of the hunter and she found that suddenly much more exciting than worrying. She wanted to touch him, to be in his arms again.

'Are you sure?' she said, feeling a rush of euphoria.

He grinned, let his eyes flick downwards once. 'Very sure.'

'But you've just got through being *un*conventional,' she said as he drew her closer to the bed.

'You want proof?' He yanked her down onto his towelling-clad body and irrefutable proof. And this time, it was Ami's caresses that brought inarticulate little sounds to the articulate North Kendrick's lips. It was her hands and her mouth that stroked and fondled and encompassed until he sighed and begged—'Yes, yes—no, no, stop!' And when she laughed in triumph at her power over him, he rolled over and spread her on the soft, quilted bed and covered her body, filled it with his so that she couldn't think at all, only feel as they combined their power to climb the heights.

Eventually they lay together, lazily loving. North nuzzled her ear, said, 'Conventional enough for you?'

Positively primitive, she thought, as small shivers of completion still rippled on her skin. 'Very civilised,' she said demurely.

North was gone in the morning. He'd left a dozen red roses on the pillow next to her, with a note. Smiling lazily, Ami opened the envelope, wondering how many men could lay their hands on a dozen dewy red roses on a Sunday morning. He would probably appear through the doorway in a moment with fresh-baked croissants and brewed coffee.

'Darling,' the note began in large, hasty script. *Darling*. Ami's smile widened and she lay back on the pillows and closed her eyes dreamily for a moment, the note held to her chest. Her first love letter from him. She felt like a schoolgirl.

'The second newspaper has cancelled, so the widow Anderson is no longer required.'

Ami sat up, frowning at this unloverlike tone.

'Something urgent has come up and I have to fly to UK for a few days. Damned awful timing. Keep Wednesday night free for me. North. P.S. Last night was wonderful.'

She turned the note over, hoping for something more. But it was no love letter in spite of the postscript, she thought wryly. Ami picked up the roses and breathed in their perfume, aware of a niggle of disquiet. Words had always been important to her. She could pick up a page of script and an innocuous phrase would leap out at her, seemingly more significant than the rest. But she reread the note and failed to identify the part that was bothering her. It was just, she decided, that she was disappointed not to see North today when she was filled with tenderness for him. Flushed with the pleasures of last night, she wanted to look at him over breakfast, touch his hand, share the look of lovers who knew each other intimately. But North had gone north. She laughed softly. 'I love you, North,' she said to the roses, then phoned Harry to tell him she was going home, as she and her disguise were no longer needed.

'Come on up before you go,' he said. 'I'll send the lift for you.'

There was some delay with the private elevator but eventually Ami was delivered to the penthouse, her eyes averted from the mirrored lift walls. One look at her and she felt certain that Harry would know she had been cavorting all night with his son.

As she stepped into the penthouse foyer, she heard a woman's voice, rising and fading as if she was walking about facing one way, then another. Francesca's voice, full of gaiety and archness and raised as it always was when she spoke to Harry, convinced as she was that all elderly people were deaf. 'I shouldn't be saying anything because we're keeping it quiet just yet, Harry, but North must have already told *you*—' Ami caught the word *divorce* loud and clear, then an indistinct jumble before the next distinguishable phrases that came so rapidly and breathlessly Ami thought the brunette must be turning pirouettes. '—second wedding—so thrilled—for keeps this time—white wedding, just like...'

'Well, congratulations. That's the best news I've heard in a long time!' Harry said and Ami flinched at the hearty approval in his voice.

'Oh, *here* it is! Thank heavens,' said Francesca. 'It's my favourite scarf, I'd hate to lose it.'

Ami backed into the lift, driven to escape before Francesca could appear, wafting that filmy, tiger-striped scarf like a victory pennant. *Second wedding.* She felt quite calm as the doors silently closed and she glanced at her reflection. No secrets to be seen in the inscrutable face that looked back at her. *North must have already told you.*

From her suite she phoned Harry and said she had to go, would see him later. Still in a numbed state of calm, she left, picked up Spritz from the kennels and went home, did her chores, washed the car, mowed the grass.

The widow Anderson is no longer required. Ami pushed the mower to cut another straight swathe on the half-mown lawn. She turned for the return trip and yanked the heavy mower around with sudden savagery. It was a hot day and she hadn't bothered with gardening gloves and her hands were already developing sore spots, but the hurt inside her was so bad, she only faintly registered the lesser pain. She had been so sure she could trust North. So sure there was something special between them. There had been moments when she felt a wordless communication in him. The time in that gaudy suite, was it only two days ago? She'd looked at him and he at her and she could have *sworn* that... 'Agh!' Her guttural rasp of pain and humiliation was masked by the racket of the motor mower. She gritted her teeth. What had she thought it was? A moment of cosmic recognition? A meaningful meeting of two souls? '*Ha!*'

She traversed the length of the garden again with escalating speed and scant attention to the task in hand, not caring that her normally straight mowing lines were wandering. Perhaps, she thought, in pathetic hopefulness, there was some explanation? The North she had come to know was not such a louse, surely? Maybe Francesca had misinterpreted something he'd said. Ami pondered the idea as she tore up and down the garden, watching the lush summer growth of grass and flowering weed emerge flat and uniform from beneath the blades. North might be a manipulative, compulsive winner but he surely had more style than that. More integrity. More sincerity.

But he was a man who was used to planning his strategies. One of the reasons he had survived a harsh financial climate when others had gone under was his willingness to wait for his investments to yield fruit. So maybe all that style and integrity and sincerity she thought she had discovered in him were just another Kendrick manouvre. All that charm, all that romantic hand-kissing nonsense had been a mood-setting strategy.

She turned off the mower. There were blisters on her hands. The lawn was chewed up, bare in patches, and she realised she had forgotten to adjust the height of the blades. The overspill of grass from the catcher lay in little, crooked lines, showing where she had departed from the straight and narrow. She should have listened to Emma. She should never have gone and walked on North Kendrick's turf.

CHAPTER TEN

A PARCEL, bearing the stamp of a classy jeweller, arrived at the shop on Monday. In a velvet box was a silver bracelet to match the ones Ami so often wore, but this one was studded with diamonds.

'It's fantastic,' Helen breathed, looking over her shoulder. 'You're not sending it back!' she exclaimed, when Ami repackaged it.

'Absolutely,' she said. 'I only opened it to see—' To see just how wonderful he had judged the other night. Her face flamed as she scrawled North's name and the hotel address on the wrapping. Had his executive gift-buying service organised this little token from him? Was this by way of reimbursement for a willing lover? She felt cheap and degraded.

'You toss his orchids in the bin and send his diamonds back! Most women would give their eyeteeth to be in your position.'

'I'm very attached to my eyeteeth.' If it was only a matter of eyeteeth, she thought wryly. She had given too much of greater importance. Her self-respect. Her love. Besides, many women probably *had* been in her position—ex-lover, ex-ornament in North Kendrick's life. The only offering he could make was material, which was why Francesca really was the perfect partner for him. She felt a certain strength flow back when she realised that nothing had changed. So, she had confirmed that North was a manipulative bastard—she'd always known that. So, she had made love with him. She was a grown woman and everyone was entitled to one big affair, one big mistake. So, it was a fleeting romance, all over. It

162

was best that way. Even if North loved her, he was not for her. He liked his champagne cold and his women beautiful. She had to know that the man in her life appreciated those things about her that would last, not just the outward things that by chance pleased him right now. She refused to be like Francesca, checking in every reflective surface, fearing her looks had diminished and her lovableness with them. Poor Francesca. She worked hard to pity the woman who would have North for a while, at least.

She received a message from North via his secretary on Wednesday. 'Mr. Kendrick regrets he has been delayed in negotiations in London and can't make your appointment this evening,' she told Ami.

'Surprise, surprise!' Ami drawled.

Disconcerted, the woman said, 'He'll, er, be in touch soon.'

To retrieve some shred of self-respect, she spent that night composing a letter to North. She was darned if she would play the part of the starry-eyed lover, the last to know that it was all over.

'Dear North,' she wrote. 'It is with great difficulty that I write this.' That at least was the truth. 'We have had a turbulent relationship since our first meeting and it was inevitable I suppose that we would make love eventually. I was attracted to you from the start and I know it was mutual. The other night was extremely pleasurable. I will remember it fondly,' she wrote, her hand clenched into a claw on the pen as she strove for the tone of the liberated woman who liked her lovers but didn't want them hanging around underfoot. 'However, for me the other night was an isolated incident. I do hope we can remain friends for Harry's sake.'

After some consideration she crossed out 'extremely pleasurable' and substituted 'most enjoyable.' Why give North's ego an unnecessary boost? She copied out the final draft and sent it to his secretary with a request to

forward it on, then asked Helen to say she was out in
the unlikely circumstance that North phoned the shop.
Her phone rang once or twice at home in the evening,
but she didn't answer it. Another dozen roses, yellow
this time, arrived at the shop with a card that said,
'Missing you. North.' She gave them to Helen. A week
later a bouquet of November lilies arrived. 'Thinking of
you. Love, North.'

   Love, North. The words leapt from the card, almost
fluorescent with significance. Ami wanted to believe it.
Holding the flowers, she felt the treacherous leap of
hope. Maybe he wasn't just playing games. Maybe he
really did care, really did miss her and think of her. But
there was Francesca. What was she going to do? she
thought, unable for the first time in her life to think her
problems through clearly. Was he an unprincipled swine
or not? *Love, North.* The words echoed in her head,
scattering reason. And to stop herself mooning she forced
herself to consider an obvious reason for this continued
courting. North might have in mind an affair to run
concurrently with his engagement and eventual marriage. It helped her work up a nice feeling of outrage
and she plunked the exotic flowers in Helen's arms.

   Harry moved out of the Avalon, back to his own
house. By way of compromise, he had allowed North to
arrange a weekly call from a nurse-helper. Ami gathered
that Harry had planned on training a nice young woman
to his own way of thinking. As North had hired a crew-
cut male nurse-helper with muscles, a tattoo and a
motorbike, Harry was enlivened by a new challenge. The
old man phoned Ami several times, anxious over his
Christmas plans. His daughter and her family were
coming from Melbourne to stay with him. 'I had one
hell of a free-for-all with North over it,' he said with the
relish of a winner. 'Had to promise to get The Ter-
minator in to help with the arrangements. He had the

family Santa suit dry-cleaned and bought me one of those fold-up Christmas trees—I suppose it'll have to do.'

Ami's parents planned to fly to Tasmania to Lenore's sister for the celebration. 'I wish you'd come with us,' her mother said. 'I hate to think of you stuck in Sydney alone for Christmas.'

'I won't be alone,' Ami assured her. 'I've heaps of invitations.'

One from Harry, to join him and his family on Christmas Eve, and she wasn't likely to accept that. One from Emma and Matt, and only an insensitive clod would intrude on the first Christmas of newlyweds. One from Helen, for drinks in her starry-windowed lounge. Several from friends. Heaps of invitations.

As December heated up, Ami sold dozens of her light-weight tropical Santa beards and eyebrows. Sydney's Christmas lights were switched on, the city's buildings were decked with holly, Santas, reindeer and ropes of flashing lights. A giant Christmas tree went up in Martin Place, and the flower sellers' stalls were stocked with Christmas bells and bronze-red flowering native Christmas bush. Silver and gold stars everywhere. At the Avalon, Ami saw as she passed once, the lollipop trees were tastefully hung with bauble-like red apples and the pots were swathed in Victorian-style garlands. Morgan had a sprig of holly in his lapel. Not a garish Santa, reindeer or flashing light to be seen. No stars. Home to heaven.

Ami assumed North must have received her letter and cancelled any further tributes with Monica's gift-buying service, which was just as well because Helen's husband had flown into a jealous rage when she kept taking flowers home. Ami wondered if North would be putting on the family Santa suit. She imagined him dressed in it, a pillow tied around his middle, heaving a sack of toys for his nieces and nephews. Lousy, manipulative, selfish, chauvinistic Uncle North. His lashes would be impossibly thick and black for a Santa. His teeth impossibly white. Shoulders athletically broad. 'And what do you want for Christmas, Ami Winterburn...'

Peace on Earth.

Goodwill to all.

Amnesia.

Ho, ho, ho.

Sales slackened off at the shop as the schools performed their end-of-year plays and wound down for the summer holidays. She threw herself into a reorganisation of the shop, and fell off a ladder while clearing a top shelf at the shop. Her weaker ankle was badly sprained, and she spent two days resting it. Her mother, who had nursed Ami's weak ankle through years of ballet, insisted on sending someone from the agency to cook, clean the house and answer the phone. Her mother also sent magazines, and in one of them was an article about Francesca entitled, 'The Second Time Around.' She tossed it aside but the photograph of the fashion designer in the arms of her man landed upside down on the carpet and Ami couldn't resist a peek. But even before she turned the picture right way up, she could see the man was not North. Ami frowned, seized the magazine. 'Fashion designer Francesca Parelli, marrying for the second time next month, will have a hard time finding the traditional "something new." She will be married in the church where she was first married, will wear the same dress and be attended by the same bridesmaids. Even the groom will be the same.'

'What?' Ami read it again, attempting to hold back an idiotic pleasure that Francesca's bridegroom was losing his hair and had a moustache.

'Francesca and Antony will celebrate their reunion after a six-month separation by renewing their vows. "This time," Francesca says, snuggling up to her first and second husband, "it is for keeps."'

Ami gave an embarrassed laugh, mortified that she'd so badly interpreted a fragment of conversation yet relieved that North had not lied to her after all. Her intuition had been right. He wasn't the kind of man to propose to one woman and sweep another off her feet all within twenty-four hours. The news Francesca had been dying to tell him that night was not that she and her husband were to be divorced, but remarried. Ami felt a surge of spirits that waned as she remembered the letter she had sent him. Biting her lip, she wished she had waited a little longer before mailing it. But on reflection, she decided it was just as well.

It was a warm, wet night a week before Christmas when she gave her last class for the year at the Shoelace Theatre. To protect her ankle, she made use of some stage crutches to move between the students as they emulated her make-up techniques. Once again, she had demonstrated first on her own face.

'I can't believe you can look so gross,' one of her students said as the lesson drew to a close. 'Ugly as sin—on your left side, anyway.'

'Beauty is only skin deep,' Ami said with a horrible grin.

The subject tonight had been distortion, the ruined Phantom of the Opera face, and she had disfigured one side of her face, closed one eye to a mere slit and drawn the lid downward, puckered her skin, twisted her mouth and slashed a horrible, partly healed scar across one cheekbone.

'Beards and moustaches next week,' she told them as they cleared away their equipment to leave. 'Bring photos and false hair for practice.'

They left and she stacked the chairs, gathered up the waste tissues in a bin, turned off all but the nominal lighting in the auditorium. Before she could remove her make-up, she heard a door shut and footsteps in the auditorium. She went through the wings onto the half-lit stage. 'Is that you, Mr McShane?' she called, looking around the rows of seats for the security guard.

'No.'

Her heart flipped. She followed the voice, saw North over to her left. He looked marvellous and she drank in those details of his presence available to her, like a woman offered drink in the desert. The dark hair, glistening with raindrops, the handsome nose, shadowed and emphasized by the side lighting, the contours of his lean cheeks. He wore dark jeans and a shiny black rain jacket with the collar turned up. His hands were thrust into the pockets as he stared broodingly at the stage from the tiered auditorium.

'You look like a movie bad guy,' she said with a nervous laugh.

'You typecast me long ago,' he said dryly. 'How's your leg? I only found out about your accident last week. Harry told me you were in hospital but were okay now.'

'How did he know?' she said inanely, as if she cared when North was standing out there alongside row M.

'He phoned your place and spoke to a nurse or someone.'

'Oh,' she said. A deep silence ensued. Hospital? she thought. She'd only been in the casualty ward, where Helen had frantically taken her, for a few hours to X-ray for fractures. North stayed where he was, leaning on the seat beside him so that his body took on a sideways slant.

'I have been trying to get in touch with you ever since—'

He stopped short and she wondered just what phrase he would use to describe the occasion. Ever since our one-night stand? Evern since I left a dozen roses in my place and ran out?

'You could have written,' she said stroppily.

'I don't express myself well in writing,' he said.

'You made your meaning very plain in the one note you left for me.'

'Did I?' he said harshly. 'That's more than I can say of that piece of hypocritical, pseudo-feminist garbage you sent me.'

'*Your* note was more in the nature of an interoffice memo—"the widow Anderson is no longer required. Please keep Wednesday night free,"' she mimicked in a deep voice. 'You only managed to remember how *wonderful* our night together had been in the postscript!'

He moved down to row K, the raindrops on his hair and jacket turning red as he passed a neon exit sign.

'I could have said our night together was "most enjoyable,"' he said through gritted teeth. 'I could have said I'd remember it "fondly."'

'Well,' she said, flushing slightly. 'It's true.'

'Don't you bloody *dare* remember it fondly.'

'You're a powerful man but you can't dictate my memories.'

'I will *not* be remembered *fondly*!' he said louder. 'Like a—a discarded teddy bear!'

She laughed but North stared at her with a thwarted expression. He was serious, she thought, swallowing hard. Her heartbeat raced.

'When I got that letter,' he said deliberately, 'I thought, to hell with her. Stop trying to phone her every night and every day. Stop sending flowers. Stop thinking about her. Don't see her again.' He flicked a descending raindrop from his forehead with a small, violent gesture, added with self-contempt, 'But here I am.'

'Um, I was upset when I wrote that letter. I heard that Francesca was getting married again and I thought it was to you, and that you'd lied to me about your involvement with her so that I would, er...'

There was a visible straightening of his spine as if he'd been given an infusion of confidence. His hands came out of his pockets, went to his hips, pushed back the black jacket. Ami hastily reviewed what she'd said to account for this sudden power swing in his favour.

'You thought I made love to you while I was planning to marry Fran?' he said, shaking his head. 'You really do have me cast as the villain, don't you?'

'I'm sorry,' she said, shrugging. 'But you have to admit that basically, what I wrote is true. I mean, you and I—we—well, it's a physical thing, really, and very nice, but—'

'Very nice? Very bloody *nice*?' he roared. 'I don't know what you feel for me, but I love you, Ami Winterburn, I love you.'

It sounded like a declaration of war rather than a declaration of love. But the phrase echoed around beneath the rafters, proving that the expense of acoustic linings had been warranted. Ami Winterburn, I love you. A couplet sweet as any Shakespeare had written.

'Well—*say* something!'

Her heartbeat was deafening. 'I—I—' she croaked and he seemed to find something encouraging in her stuttering response.

He cut down through row E to the centre aisle, moving fast, below her now, a man with a sense of purpose. He was powering towards the stage when he looked up at her again and stopped, horror on his face. 'Ami—oh, my God, Ami darling—the accident— Harry didn't tell me.'

He stood stock-still, his face working. His nostrils flared. '*You* didn't tell me,' he accused, pointing a finger at her. 'Why the hell didn't you tell me?'

Ami gaped at him. She put a hand to the artificially distorted side of her face, visible now to him. North was talking about that, staring at it in—what? Revulsion? Loathing? Panic? She saw the pallor in his face, and the blood drained from her own head. North thought her face had been injured in the accident, too. She watched him absorb this new, hideous image of her and waited in a fatalistic calm. Perhaps he was already discovering that he couldn't love her, after all. North preferred his women beautiful.

'Imagine waking next to a face like this,' she said, making a stab at a light-hearted tone. In a moment she would have to tell him it wasn't genuine. And that would be worse still. She wondered what would hurt him the most—his horror at her ruined face or his relief that it was a fake. 'I'm afraid this face doesn't meet your high aesthetic standards, North,' she said in a high, strained voice.

White patches showed beside his mouth. 'High aesthetic standards! You make me sound like a bloody quality control officer or something.' North's eyes narrowed on her suddenly as a suspicion struck him. 'Hell,' he said, clapping a hand to his forehead. 'I've fallen for it again.' He ground his teeth then strode across the auditorium to a side door. Ami heard the stamp of his footsteps up the steps, across a concrete apron, traversing the control console until they echoed on the stage itself. She turned awkwardly to confront him. North glared at the left side of her face. He ran a fingertip over the texture of it. 'All your own work, of course,' he said tautly.

She nodded.

'So it is just your ankle that you injured—you're not hurt otherwise?'

'I only fell off a ladder,' she said. 'And the reason you only heard about it yesterday was because it only happened yesterday.'

'What? Harry said—I got the impression it was more serious, that you'd been laid up in hospital for a week.' He gave a dry laugh. 'That old meddler, playing cupid, I suppose.' He hauled her close, suddenly angry again. 'I should have realised you wouldn't be walking around with week-old injuries like this, but logic deserts me where you're concerned.' And he kissed her with savage

passion, bending her backwards beneath the force of it.
His hands swept over her back in a rough caress, spread
on her rear, tilting her more intimately against him. Ami
gasped, dropped one of the crutches and it clattered un-
heeded to the floor. It was so long since she'd been in
his arms, smelled the mix of fragrances and odours that
were distincively his, kissed him. Making up for lost time,
she kissed him now, feeling the friction of his teeth on
her tongue, tasting the sweetness of oranges in his mouth.
He straightened suddenly, looking at her with a glitter
of combined desire and anger in his eyes.

'So. I failed the test, I suppose,' he said harshly, under
his own breath. 'That's why you didn't tell me you were
made-up, isn't it? You thought, let's see if this man of
superficial feelings and trivial values will say he loves
me with scarred skin and a drooping eye.'

'North, it wasn't like that. I had just finished doing
a class. When you walked in I—forgot I was wearing
make-up. When you saw it you assumed it was real—'

'And you let me! Because you thought I'd run
screaming, didn't you?' He clasped her arms tightly, gave
her a small shake. 'All that stuff about wanting the entire
you, not just your lovely hide—you had to check it out,
didn't you?'

She twisted away from him, angered. 'And the fact
is, I still don't know, do I?' she snapped.

His face looked ashen in contrast to his black clothes.

'Well, then, you're going to have to work it out for
yourself, aren't you, Ami?' he said quietly. 'I don't
understand this obsession of yours.'

He stepped back, let her go, only grabbing her arm
once more for a few seconds to support her as she
wobbled. He picked up the second crutch and handed
it to her. 'I love you,' he said roughly. 'I want you so
bad I could make love to you right now, standing up,
on this stage, and I wouldn't care too much, frankly, if
there was an audience here.' Ami flushed a dark red.

'But then, I would say that, wouldn't I? Because I know you're really beautiful under that stuff and trivial, shallow types like me can't contemplate anything else,' he said in a low, guttural voice. 'I'd better leave before we have another *isolated incident.*'

He left then, retracing his steps until the sound of his leaving faded into the space of his arrival. Ami was shattered, remorseful, angry. Tears in her eyes, she removed the illusory effects from her face, not caring if she tore the flimsy pieces of latex. Was she misjudging him? She wanted to believe it, but years of accumulated fears and the many Mirandas she had known got in the way.

His mood was unsociable and he should have declined Lenore Winterburn's invitation to her harbour home to discuss the donation of a sculpture from his collection. Curiosity and a renewed hopefulness, which he refused to acknowledge, made him go. This was where Ami had lived, he thought, looking around the lovely house that was expensively but unpretentiously furnished for comfort. A cluster of photographs drew his attention, and he stopped, picked up a print of a plain, skinny little girl, all arms and legs, pushing a miniature wheelbarrow. He ran a finger over the face, smiling at that familiar, level expression in the child's eyes. 'Oh, I'm sorry,' he said, putting the photo down as he felt Ami's mother watching. He flushed. If he was not careful, he would find himself wallowing in sentiment, he thought in disgust, singing bursts of 'On the Street Where You Live.'

'Come and meet my husband,' Lenore said cosily. North was not misled. Lenore Winterburn was a shrewd, intelligent woman, sharply observant and stubborn as an ox, he guessed, once she'd made up her mind. His chances of getting away without donating a sculpture to her charity were nil. A formidable woman. Like mother, like daughter.

Steven Winterburn was in his study, a large room lined with bookshelves and hung with startling before-and-after photographs—faces smooth, faces ruined and distorted. After the formalities, North's eyes were drawn to them. He frowned. 'I thought for a moment they were photographs of Ami's work,' he said, taking a closer look.

'Mine, actually,' said her father with a smile. 'But I see what you mean.'

'Steven is a reconstructive surgeon,' Lenore said. 'These are some of his patients before and after surgery.'

North looked more carefully. Not faces ruined, but faces restored. 'I suppose Ami took on the therapeutic cosmetics because of your involvement in reconstruction,' he said, thinking hard.

'Yes. She has always been interested in my work,' her father said. 'From the time she was a little girl she would come in here and ask about the people in the photos. Not the most pleasant side of life for a child to confront,' he said dryly. 'But Ami was never the kind of child who could be fobbed off with pretty answers. She was quite critical of fairy tales, I remember.' He smiled.

'I can imagine. Snow in summer,' North said half to himself, moving from portrait to portrait.

'Quite,' Ami's father said uncertainly. 'Cosmetic therapists are few and far between—the stress of dealing with disfigured people gets to them, you see. When we lost our last one and there was no-one to refer patients to, Ami took it on. She says she copes with it okay.'

'She cries, but not in front of her students,' North said absently.

Ami's parents exchanged a speaking glance. 'You must know our daughter very well,' her father said, looking him over with a more critical eye.

'I think I know her a little better now,' he said, with a last look at the studies of faces ruined and mended. He thought of a little girl, growing up with this acute awareness of the evanescence of beauty or normality and the need to look beneath the surface. In a rush of enlightenment, he remembered something Harry had said. Joking, North had studied a stooped, lined woman passing by and said, 'Thanks to Ami, I can never see an old person anymore without wondering if there's someone young underneath.' And Harry had said, 'Don't wonder, son. There always is.'

With understanding came a feeling of helplessness that made North grind his teeth. How the hell was he going to convince Ami that he loved her, the real her? His track record didn't help him, he admitted ruefully. She loved him, he knew it, *felt* it. But she had grown up with those photographs and the small, tragic stories that went with them and she had him taped as exactly the kind of man she couldn't be with—a man with only some of his senses in working order, blind to her qualities save those that afforded him direct pleasure. Surely, she could see that might have been true once, but not any more? But she was so damned stubborn, so strong, so determined.

Before he left, he donated a nymph to Lenore's charity. Like mother, like daughter, he thought, his head reeling from the experience. He called up a four-letter word he hadn't used since early adolescence. 'Help,' he said out loud as he drove away.

A postcard came from Emma, still travelling in Europe on her honeymoon. The small space was crammed with tourist anecdotes and glowing description as well as some pithy advice. 'Regarding that supercilious swine. Don't be too hasty. Any man who can nurse you through a virus and still fancy you—and be "just good friends" with the gorgeous Francesca—is not an empty vessel. Home on twenty-third. Having a wonderful time. Do *not* wish you were here.'

Her mother phoned. 'Darling, you remember my writer? He's abandoned that book he was working on and wants someone to tap-dance in an elevator so that he can study the reactions of the occupants. Naturally, I thought of you. Your ankle's okay now, isn't it? Have you still got your tap shoes?'

'He's abandoned the *book*?' Ami shouted. 'I went and asked his stupid questions, which changed my entire *life*, and he's abandoned the *book*? No, I will not tap-dance in an elevator!'

'I see,' her mother said. 'By the way, we got our nymph.'

Ami's senses quickened. 'Oh?'

'North came to see us. Are you in love with him as much as he is with you?'

She clutched at the phone. 'What makes you think he's in love with me?'

'It must have been the way he mooned over that picture of you on the hall table. I mean, I love you dearly, Ami darling, but even I have to admit you were the plainest little thing on two legs until you were fifteen. He looked as inspired as if you were Helen of Troy. Poor man, he blushed when he saw that I noticed.'

'*Blushed*—North?'

'So you won't take the tap-dancing job?' Lenore went on aggravatingly, when Ami would have liked to hear more about this mooning, blushing North. 'I can't say I blame you. I'm not keen on elevators myself. Bye— your father and I will phone Christmas Day from Tassie.'

Ami hung up and sat a while. She picked up the phone, took a deep breath and keyed in North's office number at the Avalon. It was only a temporary arrangement and Mr. Kendrick had moved back to his customary office in Crows Nest, a woman told her. But North wasn't there, either.

Christmas Eve. Sydney's weather was sultry, the skies blue. The office parties were over. Last-minute shopping and trading. Christmas decorations were going cheap.

The Salvation Army played Christmas carols for the fortunate and prepared Christmas dinners for those less so. Cars packed high headed in slow lines across the Harbour Bridge, heading north, heading south to beaches, campgrounds, holiday houses, to Christmas reunions with parents, children, family, friends. The city's churches proclaimed the birth of the Christ child. Ami slipped into St. James, near Hyde Park, to reflect on love and hope and peace on earth. They closed the shop at noon and Ami delivered gifts to special customers and friends. She kept Harry's present till last.

Harry's house was a modest brick bungalow in an old inner-west suburb greened by mature oaks and fig trees and woody roses. Ami found a parking spot in a row of visitors' cars parked in the street and walked up a path across a lawn bordered with plumbago hedges. There was no answer to her knock and, after a while, she walked around to the back of the house. The back garden was long and narrow with the parasol canopy of a poinciana tree bearing garlands of red flowers. At the end of the garden, beneath the arching boughs, was a large shed. Its timber doors were flung wide open and, framed in the aperture, lit by bright sunlight against the dark interior, were Harry and a partly dismantled motorbike. And North. Ami felt a rush of pure delight, a sudden piercing happiness. The sight of him, on his knees, obviously doing Harry's bidding made her think of the day he'd been on his knees beside her, daubing her with antiseptic.

'No, no, *no*,' Harry was saying, shaking his head and pointing. 'The *other* one!'

'Aw, Dad—give me a chance!' North protested. He worked something loose and showed it to his father then wiped a hand across his face. 'If you're going to supervise every nut and bolt in this project, I think I'll—' He broke off as he saw Ami.

The sense of buoyancy heightened. She smiled at North, unable to keep the feeling to herself. Somewhere, in her reflections on love and hope, she had made a quantum leap past her doubts. This was right. North was right. I love you, North. He stood up slowly, eyes fixed on her face, reading the scattered clues there with all the intense speculation he had once devoted to her alphabet sweater. He wore faded overalls that were too tight over the shoulders. There were smears of dirt and grease on his face, his hair flopped over his forehead, he needed a shave. The man was a mess. He looked wonderful, strong and vibrant, a man in his prime.

'Ami Winterburn,' he said, turning her name over on his tongue as if it was the first time he'd said it. He stuck his hands on his hips but in spite of the muscular assertiveness of the pose he looked uncertain.

She walked down to them. Harry beamed a welcome at her.

'We're renovating one of my old racing bikes,' he told Ami.

'You mean *I'm* renovating your old racing bike—you're supervising,' North said with a snort.

'He's always around here lately, tinkering with stuff on the workbench. More inventing, I shouldn't wonder,' Harry said.

'*Tinkering*?' Ami looked at the bike. Not partly dismantled, after all, but partly rebuilt, which was quite different. Smiling, she looked at North as he stepped out from behind the Ducati. Her gaze came to rest, askance, on the rolled-up trouser legs of his overalls that hung incongruously over boots.

'What do you think of them?' Harry said, seeing her interest. 'The boots. I used to race in them.'

Black bike boots with straps and silver buckles. The ones North had coveted as a kid, the ones Harry had said he might grow into one day.

'I thought you gave them away to someone else, Harry!'

'I told him that, just to punish him,' Harry admitted sheepishly. 'He was thick as thieves suddenly with his science teacher—the one that took out patents for him. He didn't need me anymore, I thought. He'd left me behind, so I hid the boots away and told him I'd given them to someone else.' The old man pulled a face. 'Thought he might have grown into them at last so I gave them to him today. And what do you think—they're a perfect fit.' Harry gave his wheezing laugh and winked at Ami.

North didn't notice. His attention was on Ami, compelling her attention back to him. His grey eyes beamed a warmth her way that had nothing to do with the brilliant sunshine. It was a look she had seen many times. When she'd been dirty and scratched and dishevelled by the roadside, when she'd been sweating and sick with a virus, the last time she'd been disguised as an elderly widow, wrinkled and worn with time. At her best and at her worst he had looked at her just like this.

Harry flicked a look between North and Ami. 'Well, I've got things to do. The rest of the family are arriving about ten tonight and I still don't like that darned Christmas tree... too *glittery*, if you ask me.'

'I don't want to interrupt anything,' Ami said.

'North only called in for some advice and I've given him that,' Harry said, scarcely leaning on his stick as he walked towards the house, humming under his breath.

The screen door banged ostentatiously behind Harry. Ami looked at North. He yanked the front of the overalls and popped the studs, then peeled the faded drill down, shook it free from his booted legs. Underneath he wore a burgundy T-shirt and jeans tucked into Harry's old bike boots. He tossed the overalls aside and surveyed her, hands on hips, that hint of uncertainty about him making her heart turn over.

'You, the boy genius, asking for advice?' she said with a nervous laugh, thinking how it had put a spring in Harry's step.

'Where you're concerned I could use a panel of advisers.'

'I heard you'd donated a nymph to Mum's charity. That was generous of you.'

'*Wise*, anyway. I wouldn't want to start off on the wrong foot with my future mother-in-law.' His eyes narrowed as he assessed the effect of this breathtaking assumption.

Her heartbeat quickened. 'North, what are you saying?'

'Just that I've met the only woman I ever want—as my mother-in-law.'

'The *only* woman?'

'It's her or no-one. Do you think she'll—like the idea?'

Ami smiled brilliantly. Any minute now she was likely to pirouette around Harry's back garden. 'She'll *love* the idea.'

'You're sure about that?'

'Absolutely.'

'She'll say yes?'

'Oh, yes.'

'In that case, I'll ask her—when the time is right.'

'You weren't going to risk a no? Coward.'

'Absolutely.'

He smiled at her and she at him and it was happening again. That peculiar communication without words, a thing at once primitive and more sophisticated than any artificial means of communication devised by humanity. If Harry was peeking through his window he would see them standing metres apart but they were as close as two people could be without touching.

'I went into your father's study when I called at your house. I saw the faces of his patients in those photo studies. It made me realize how serious you are about superficiality, how you might guard against it. It seemed obsessive to me, I didn't understand, but I think I do now. I came away a desperate man, wondering if I'd ever be able to convince you that I love you—the whole you, not just the pretty bits.'

'I knew you did. It was buried deep, that's all—under fear and cowardice. I just needed time.'

'That's what Harry said, when I asked his advice. He said you loved me, that I should be patient, and wait.' North studied her carefully, folded his arms and leaned against the shed door, waiting, the picture of patience spoiled only by the growing gleam in his eyes.

'But you have to admit,' she said, reacting to his growing complacence, 'that you seemed to be all the things I always said I would avoid. For a start, you were so arrogant—'

He opened his eyes wide in surprise.

'Talking about women as if they were mere commodities in our life—all the women you met were either "too young, too old, married or feminist academics,"' she quoted.

'Ah. Yes,' he said, conceding the point with a grimace.

'You collected painting and sculptures and when you got tired of them just packed them up and sent them somewhere else. It seemed to me that you might regard women like those nymphs—nice to own for a while but replaceable. I thought I might end up like one of those torchbearers outside the Avalon, or like one of your mooning, pale pre-Raphaelite heroines.'

'Just for the record, I never tired of them. But the collection has grown so large and a southern college has been pestering me for years to turn it over to them as a public exhibition and resource for students and—' He shrugged. 'Up until a few months ago there had been a

certain lack of meaning in my life, so I decided public
works might be a good—' He stopped, struck by a
thought. 'The wheat!' he said. 'Pre-Raphaelite women—
that's what you meant.'

'Has that been bothering you?'

'When the woman of your dreams leaps naked from
your arms babbling about wheat, it causes some serious
problems for the male psyche.'

'Oh, really,' she said sceptically.

'I found myself going over that night trying to think
where it might have gone wrong and how the hell wheat
came into it. It was all a bit hazy because of the brandy.
That was true, you know.'

'If you had a hangover the next day, you were her-
oically unmoved by the sound of Ken's motorbike,' she
said dryly.

'I was so thrown, the headache the next day was the
least painful thing about it. But I kept reliving every
moment of the night that I could remember.'

'Every moment?'

'Over and over.'

'That must have been very irritating.'

'On the contrary. I found it "most enjoyable".'

She chuckled. 'In my first draft I said "extremely
pleasurable".'

His teeth flashed in a cocky grin that made her heart
bump. Ami held her arms wide and he took two giant
steps and hauled her close, held her there a moment
before he kissed her hard on the mouth. 'Woman of a
thousand faces,' he muttered into her hair. 'I love all of
them—all of you. There never will be just one face to
Ami Winterburn, will there?' He framed her face in both
hands. 'For someone supposed to be smart I can be very
slow.'

'Surely not!' she said, opening her eyes wide.

'But I finally saw it was stupid to resent you fooling
me with your Amelia disguise because that was you, too,

just in another form. You'll always be changing—growing—there'll always be a new face. I love that.'

He gathered her close and kissed her again, thoroughly. 'Ami Winterburn, I love you,' he murmured. 'And I want you...and while I could easily make love to you on a roadside or standing up on a stage, I draw the line at my father's back yard.'

Holding hands, they walked down to the house.

'Come for a drive with me and Harry?' he asked.

'I'd love to.'

'Don't you want to know where to?'

'Nope.'

'It might be a long, long way.'

'I hope it is,' she said.

It was over an hour's drive, west, straight into a blazing late afternoon sun that was dropping down towards the craggy Blue Mountains range.

'You mean you're looking for...' Harry said, as he figured out where they were going and then, 'it won't still be here. Probably got town houses built on it now. Or been turned into a mini golf course or something.'

But it hadn't been. A hand-painted sign, propped on a side road, announced Christmas Trees—Select Your Own. Down a long, dusty driveway they went, following hand-painted arrows past a house to an untidy plantation of slash pines in long grass. There were two small groups of people, one wandering about, another cutting their tree. Their voices and the ringing cuts of the axe carried on the air. Music drifted from the house.

Harry sighed. 'Fancy that—some things don't change. The same people must live here.'

'The daughter of the people we used to see,' North said.

Harry swallowed hard and said stroppily. 'Bet you didn't bring the axe.'

'It's in the boot,' North said.

Harry sighed again and got out of the car, headed off between a row of trees, slapping at a slender trunk now and then to test for some obscure quality. North stood a moment watching him, then, smiling, took out the axe and a small handsaw.

'We always cut the tree several feet above the ground. That way it doesn't die but grows again. Once, when I was fifteen, we cut our tree from the same one we'd had when I was five.'

Ami looked around at the clumping, erratic regrowth from the post-high stumps, evidence of past Christmases. She thought of North brought here as a boy by his father, choosing a tree. He watched Harry's progress, smiling slightly. 'I think we'll let Harry pick the tree. He seems to know what he's looking for.'

North hefted the axe over his shoulder, took Ami's hand. As they moved onto the rough ground between the pines he made a muffled sound and hobbled a bit. Ami looked enquiringly at him.

'Those boots—' she began.

'Don't you dare tell him they're too small,' he growled.

Ami remembered Harry's wink and laughed, her heart contracting at North's protectiveness. 'I love you,' she said. 'My mother and my best friend vouched for you, so it isn't surprising.'

'I've always believed in the superior perception of women,' he said brazenly.

'But I think it was the gardenia that did it.'

'The gardenia?'

'If it hadn't been for that I wouldn't have felt so upset about you throwing me out. But you tucked that flower in my hair so gently that it ruined my image of you as an out-and-out rotter. I doubt that I would have turned up as Amelia to gatecrash your party, if it hadn't been for the gardenia. I couldn't forgive you for it because it made you unforgettable.'

'You mean there was only a flower between me and life without Ami Winterburn? Remind me to recommend a raise for Morgan.'

The air was mauve with early dusk and shimmering still with the departed radiance of the sun. She had the strangest feeling of timelessness as she walked, her hand in North's, through the field of trees harvested, growing, regrown. The links of tradition. Parents and children. Children and parents. Christmases past. Today, this Christmas Eve. Christmases to come. 'We'll come here for our Christmas trees,' she said.

'I thought you didn't approve of all this pine-tree stuff in the land of gum trees and palms.'

Ami threw her arms wide. 'Oh, I always say that in September,' she said. 'But by December, I always come around to the idea of pine trees and summer snow.'

Harry's voice carried on the still air. 'Now that,' he said, 'is what I call a Christmas tree!'

There was some bickering between father and son as North shaped up to cut Harry's tree. Happiness, Ami thought, was something you either remembered or yearned for. Hardly ever did you recognise it at the precise moment. But this, right now—this was pure happiness, watching North heft the axe in both hands. His shoulders and back rippled as he brought the small tree down with a couple of strokes. Harry seized it and dragged it off towards the car, refusing all offers of help.

North used the saw to neaten the cut. The dusk deepened and the first star appeared in the sky. He threw down the saw and looked at it a while with Ami. Then he held his arms wide, and where else would she go except into them? 'I love you, North,' she said, wrapping her arms around his neck as she kissed him. It was too far away to be possible but Ami thought she heard a wheezy kind of laughter. Her eyes closed. 'Fifteen,' she said, after a while.

'Fifteen what?'

'Stars. Or was it sixteen? I lost count.'

He smiled, looking deep in her eyes. 'Just have to start again.'

Ami sighed. 'Darling North. That sounds most enjoyable.'

BRIDE'S
BAY RESORT

UNLOCK THE DOOR TO GREAT ROMANCE
AT BRIDE'S BAY RESORT

Join Harlequin's new across-the-lines series, set
in an exclusive hotel on an island off the coast of
South Carolina.

Seven of your favorite authors will bring you exciting stories
about fascinating heroes and heroines discovering love at
Bride's Bay Resort.

Look for these fabulous stories coming to a store near you
beginning in January 1996.

Harlequin American Romance #613 in January
Matchmaking Baby by Cathy Gillen Thacker

Harlequin Presents #1794 in February
Indiscretions by Robyn Donald

Harlequin Intrigue #362 in March
Love and Lies by Dawn Stewardson

Harlequin Romance #3404 in April
Make Believe Engagement by Day Leclaire

Harlequin Temptation #588 in May
Stranger in the Night by Roseanne Williams

Harlequin Superromance #695 in June
Married to a Stranger by Connie Bennett

Harlequin Historicals #324 in July
Dulcie's Gift by Ruth Langan

Visit Bride's Bay Resort each month wherever
Harlequin books are sold.

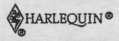

HARLEQUIN ®

BBAYG

Harlequin Romance ®

brings you

How the West Was Wooed!

Harlequin Romance would like to welcome you
Back to the Ranch again in 1996 with our new
miniseries, **Hitched!** We've rounded up twelve of our
most popular authors, and the result is a whole year
of romance, Western-style. Every month we'll be
bringing you a spirited, independent woman whose
heart is about to be lassoed by a rugged, handsome,
one-hundred-percent cowboy!

Watch for books branded **Hitched!** in the coming
months. We'll be featuring all your favorite
writers including, **Patricia Knoll, Ruth Jean Dale,
Rebecca Winters and Patricia Wilson,** to mention
a few!

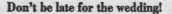

HARLEQUIN PRESENTS®

Ever felt the excitement of a dangerous desire...?

The thrill of a feverish flirtation...?

Passion is guaranteed with the seventh in our new selection of sensual stories.

Indulge in...

Dangerous Liaisons
Falling in love is a risky affair!

The Sister Swap by Susan Napier
Harlequin Presents #1788

Acclaimed author of *The Cruellest Lie*

It began as a daring deception....
But Anne hadn't bargained on living next door to
Hunter Lewis—a man who wanted to know *everything*
about her!

Still, Anne managed to keep up her act for a while. Until she
realized that hiding the truth from Hunter meant that she
was also hiding from love!

Available in January wherever Harlequin books are sold.

Harlequin Romance ®

brings you

HOLDING HER★ OUT FOR A

Some men are worth waiting for!

Beginning in January, Harlequin Romance will be
bringing you some of the world's most eligible men.
They're handsome, they're charming, but, best of all,
they're single! Twelve lucky women are about to
discover that finding Mr. Right is not a problem—it's
holding on to him!

In the coming months, watch for our Holding Out for
a Hero flash on books by some of your favorite
authors, including LEIGH MICHAELS, JEANNE ALLAN,
BETTY NEELS, LUCY GORDON and REBECCA WINTERS!

HOFH-G

A family feud...
A dangerous deception...
A secret love...

DESTINY

by Sara Wood

An exciting new trilogy from a
well-loved author...featuring romance,
revenge and secrets from the past.

Join Tanya, Mariann and Suzanne—three very special
women—as they search for their destiny. But their
journeys to love have very different results, as each
encounters the irresistible man of her dreams....

Coming next month:

Book 1—*Tangled Destinies*
Harlequin Presents #1790

Tanya had always idolized Istvan...well, he *was* her brother,
wasn't he? But at a family wedding, Tanya discovered a
dangerous secret...Istvan wasn't related to her at all!

Harlequin Presents: you'll want to know what happens next!

Available in January wherever Harlequin books are sold.